FLY AWAY

EMERALD CITY

JEN TALTY

JUPITER PRESS

This book is a work of fiction. Names, characters, places, and incidents are products of the author's imagination or used fictitiously. Any resemblance to actual events or locales or persons living or dead is entirely coincidental.

FLY AWAY

THE EMERALD CITY SERIES

Troy's Story
Book 3

USA Today Bestselling Author
JEN TALTY

the NYS Troopers series." *Long and Short Reviews*

"*In Two Weeks* hooks the reader from page one. This is a fast paced story where the development of the romance grabs you emotionally and the suspense keeps you sitting on the edge of your chair. Great characters, great writing, and a believable plot that can be a warning to all of us." *Desiree Holt, USA Today Bestseller*

"*Dark Water* delivers an engaging portrait of wounded hearts as the memorable characters take you on a healing journey of love. A mysterious death brings danger and intrigue into the drama, while sultry passions brew into a believable plot that melts the reader's heart. Jen Talty pens an entertaining romance that grips the heart as the colorful and dangerous story unfolds into a chilling ending." *Night Owl Reviews*

"This is not the typical love story, nor is it the typical mystery. The characters are well rounded and interesting." *You Gotta Read Reviews*

"Murder in Paradise Bay is a fast-paced romantic thriller with plenty of twists and turns to keep you guessing until the end. You won't want to miss this one..." *USA Today bestselling author Janice Maynard*

Troy Bowie has no desire to do anything but fly the friendly skies at twice the speed of sound. The only relationship he's ever wanted is one with the military. His career means more to him than anything —except his family. And he does whatever he can to be there for his parents and his siblings whenever possible. So, when the Navy gives him a few weeks off to attend his niece's christening, he takes it. He loves being at home—at least, for short periods— but after a few days, he's ready to get back into the cockpit of a fighter jet and go wherever the military needs him most.

Until he meets an intriguing young woman with a broken heart and decides to help her put it back together before he leaves for his next deployment.

As a Navy brat, Priela Sloane traveled all over the globe—a lifestyle she valued but not something she wanted for herself. She cut a deal with her father and served her time in the military before heading off to culinary school. Now finally on her own, Priela wants nothing to do with strong, alpha males. And she sure as hell doesn't want to date a fighter pilot. All the military ever did for her was destroy the only person she ever loved: her brother. However, Troy isn't a typical Navy man, nor does he come from a typical family, and he keeps breaking down her defenses and proving all her theories wrong.

At the end of his leave, will she let him fly away, or will she fly away with him?

For all the men and woman who serve in the armed forces.

Troy Bowie stared down at the fog lifting off Puget Sound and smiled. He loved coming home, especially in the spring when the thick, lush trees filled out the islands. As a kid, it had always reminded him of a wild jungle coming to life in a storybook. He dreamed of going on his own adventure. His father used to tease him that he had his head in the clouds and that's exactly where Troy wanted to end up, quite literally.

"You make for a shitty passenger, you know that?" his buddy, Dustin Foust, said.

"And you're a crappy pilot." Troy adjusted his headset and glanced at his best friend from high school. They had gone to the United States Naval Academy together, but Dustin hadn't lasted more than six years after graduation before leaving the military. Though it wasn't because he couldn't cut it.

Absolutely not. Dustin had been the best of the best. The true elite.

However, he'd fallen in love, and Nova couldn't cope with being a Navy wife. So, Dustin resigned and became a private pilot for a charter company to the rich and famous. It wasn't a bad gig. It paid well, and Dustin got to fly, which was cool.

But it wasn't at double the speed of sound, nor could this pretty bird go upside down.

Troy preferred pushing planes to their limits— as well as his body. He lived to serve his country. Nothing made him happier, and when he wanted the comforts of a woman, he didn't have any trouble finding one. His only concern was that whomever he chose for his bed partner understood he wasn't relationship material.

Dustin, on the other hand, had settled for the conventions of what society said he was supposed to do, and maybe he was blissfully happy, but that life wasn't for Troy. He didn't see how he could ever settle down. He'd watched his older brother and baby sister do it, and it worked for them, but Troy had a soul that needed adventure and a heart that did understand love.

"And this is a shitty-ass plane." Troy adjusted himself in the cockpit, itching to take over the controls. His buddy was right. He sucked at letting others fly. About the only thing with an engine he could relinquish control of was his little sister's sailboat, and that was only when she cut the engine and raised the sails, allowing Mother Nature to take over.

"Bite your tongue. I own this bad boy."

"Seriously?"

Dustin smiled like a big kid. "That's my big news. I started my own company. I have three planes. It's scary as shit, but I finally did it. I went out on my own, and I'm living the dream."

"That's my sister's line." Troy wanted to tell him that if he were actually living the dream, he'd still be doing Mach 2 in a Super Hornet, but why make the man feel bad? He had a wife, a kid, and another on the way. If this was what Dustin wanted now, who was Troy to rain on his parade? To each his own. Hell, his brother Jag thought cleaning a dirty diaper at three in the morning was the most exhilarating thing on the planet.

"Well, congratulations, man. That's awesome,

and I think it calls for a celebration." Troy tightened his harness.

"Oh. No. Don't you even think about it."

"Come on. Are you telling me you've never done it on one of these small jets?"

"I have not. I could get grounded."

"That'll never happen," Troy said while waggling his brows. "I'll tell them you were in the head, and it was all me."

"You will not, and we're not going to do it." Dustin reached across the cockpit and tapped one of the controls. "We're not kids anymore."

"I did a flyby just the other day."

"Okay. I rescind my statement. *I'm* not a kid anymore. Besides, even small airports like this one get their feathers in a tizzy, and I'm a new business. The last thing I need is to be on the outs with air traffic control at one of these small airports or with the FAA."

Troy held his hands up as if someone were holding a gun to his head. "Fine. No flyby. Boy, you're no fun." It took every ounce of energy Troy had not to push his buddy hard. Everything in life was meant to be challenged, and Troy didn't take no for an answer very often. If he had, he wouldn't be where he was in life.

His father hadn't been too keen on the idea of him going to the Naval Academy. It wasn't that the old man had anything against the military, but he wanted one of his boys to go to his alma mater. The more his father suggested it, the more Troy fought back.

"Are you going to be able to find time to come over for dinner? Nova would love to see you." Dustin turned his head.

"Right. Because she likes me so much."

Dustin laughed. "You're the one with a stick up your ass, not her. And for the record, she does like you, but you're always getting on my case about the Navy. That was your dream, not mine. For me, it was a means to an end, and I always thought I'd made that clear."

Christ. Troy couldn't stand to listen to this conversation again. It wasn't that he didn't like Nova; it was that she'd changed Dustin. Or maybe Dustin had changed because of her. Whatever the case, his best friend was no longer the man who'd once shared all his hopes and dreams with Troy.

"Crystal clear," Troy said as the plane approached the runway at a small private airport in Coupeville on Whidbey Island. "She rides nice."

"That she does." With the skill of a master,

Dustin set the bird down with ease. "It might not be the adrenaline rush that you get when you fly, but I still love it. And now that I own my own company, I can pick and choose the flights I want and the clientele I want. For example, I do a fair amount of work for Darcie's husband."

"My sister told me." Troy's brother-in-law, Reid, had his own company and was currently finishing up a megadeal with firefighters and smoke jumpers across the country for his state-of-the-art fire-resistant equipment. "He did mention something about you flying him back and forth to Colorado, but he didn't say it was through your own company."

"The first couple of times it was with my previous employer, but he switched to my airline when I opened it. He was actually my first contract."

"Reid's a good man," Troy said. "I can't believe my kid sister's going to be a mom. Blows my mind, you know."

"I do." Dustin turned and smiled. "But she's never looked happier."

Troy had to agree and while he was thrilled for his sister, he couldn't relate. "Well, I appreciate you picking me up. I know Hawaii isn't exactly around the corner."

"Anything for you, man, though you would have been a lot more comfortable in the back where you could have stretched out and taken a nap."

"I liked right here with you just fine."

Dustin pulled the jet next to a gassing station as directed by the ground crew. "Who's meeting you here?"

"Darcie and Reid. I'm staying with them. Much easier than staying with my parents. They won't judge me when I don't come home one night."

"Or the whole week." Dustin laughed. "Have you thought about giving up the singles' lifestyle?"

"Hell, no. The idea of being in a relationship that lasts longer than my leave makes me break out in hives."

"That's just so pathetic."

Troy unhooked himself from the seat and climbed out of the cockpit. "Gee, thanks." But he understood what his longtime friend meant. Traditional conventions dictated that a thirty-year-old man should consider—if he wasn't already—finding the right woman to settle down with and start a family.

That wasn't part of Troy's DNA. He loved the idea of family and would do anything for his parents or siblings. But he wouldn't give up his career. No, not ever, not for anyone. Sure, some marriages survived the demanding schedules and lifestyles required of military families, but it always came at a cost, especially when it came to children.

"I'll give you a call in a day or two." He gave Dustin a big bro hug.

Dustin opened the exit door. "We'll have Kyle, Crystal, and his family over for dinner, too."

"Perfect. I'd love that." Troy snagged his rucksack and tossed it over his shoulder before climbing down the stairs.

"Troy!" His sister waved from behind the fence. Reid stood next to her with his arm looped around her waist, her growing belly stretching out her shirt.

He jogged toward Darcie. "Look at my little sis with a baby bump."

She ran a hand over her stomach. "It's more like a flipping mountain." She gave him a big bear hug, planting a kiss on his cheek. "I can't believe you're here for a whole two weeks."

"I promised Jag and Callie that I'd give them all my leave if they waited to christen that cutie of theirs until I had some time when I could come home. God, I can't wait to meet my niece."

Darcie reached up and pinched his cheek. "You're the sweetest."

"You're turning into Mom." He batted her hand away.

"Why would you say that? Because I complimented you?" Darcie scowled.

"No." Troy glanced between his sister and Reid. "Because you grabbed my face like I was a kid or something. Mom does shit like that, and it drives all of us nuts."

"Well, jeez. Sorry, I thought it was nice you were home."

Reid laughed. "I wouldn't say things like that if you want to live to see tomorrow." He stretched out his hand.

Because of Troy's career, he hadn't been able to get to know his brother-in-law as well as he would have liked, but from what little time he'd spent with Reid, Troy liked him—especially since he supported Darcie and her dreams in life.

This time around.

Besides, his parents adored Reid. If the folks had given their stamp of approval, it meant he was a keeper.

"She gets a little testy because—"

"I can speak for myself, thank you," Darcie interrupted her husband, giving him a good poke in the biceps.

Reid held up his hands and mouthed, *Hormones*.

Troy bit his tongue. Growing up, the one thing Darcie hated more than anything was being treated differently because she was a girl. Not that he was doing that. However, she might take it that way.

"You're on thin ice, Reid." Darcie let out an exasperated sigh. "I do like being pregnant."

"I know you do." Reid looped his arm over her shoulders and kissed her temple.

"So, what's on the agenda for the evening?" Troy asked. "A quiet family dinner? Or did Mom end up getting her way, and there's some big surprise party waiting for me?" Troy strolled toward the parking lot. Out of habit, he took out his sunglasses and placed them over his eyes, only to shove them up on top of his head. He glanced at the sky. There was no chance the sun would be peeking out today.

And even though it wasn't raining, there was a chill in the air that felt like a combination of cold water and air-conditioning. In the summer, Seattle was the most beautiful place on Earth.

The rest of the year, well, it was still gorgeous, just not in the way anyone who didn't live there could appreciate. This was when the old saying *beauty is only skin-deep* really picked up a deeper meaning. Besides the rich history that filled the area, all the little ports and islands only added to Puget Sound's ambiance.

If Troy lived long enough to retire from the Navy, he knew this was where he'd end up. It helped that everyone in his family lived within a fifty-mile radius.

"A nice dinner at our place." Darcie yanked open the passenger door of her shiny new white SUV.

So family-like, and a little weird for him to see his sister drive, but he'd get used to it, just like he got used to the idea of Jag being the chief of police on Whidbey Island.

Troy glanced over his shoulder and laughed when he saw Nova greeting Dustin as he tried to hide her behind the plane. "Wonderful. And how big is this nice dinner at your place?" Troy climbed into the back seat. "And don't try to keep up with the ruse."

"Fine. But you better act surprised. Got it?" Darcie waggled her finger. "About fifty of your closest friends."

"Shit. Does Mom think I'm going to retire?"

"No. She's just trying to fix you up with a nice girl," Darcie said.

"Double shit." Troy closed his eyes. This was the last thing he needed while on leave. "Does she have someone in mind? Wait, let me rephrase. Who do I need to offend tonight?"

Reid burst out laughing. "Ziggy has already been laying the groundwork, and your mom, bless her kind heart, is threatening to duct tape her mouth shut if she doesn't stop trying to sabotage her efforts."

"You know, maybe if you made it a little clearer to Mom and Dad that you weren't ever getting married or having kids, they might let up."

"I've told them that if I were ever to marry, it wouldn't be until I was at least in my fifties, and only because the Navy kicked my sorry ass out for some crazy shit." He rubbed his temples as a slow headache built from the inside out. As much as his family was at the center of his universe, his mother couldn't let go of the idea that he was lonely. A concept that couldn't be further from the truth. "How many of these women will be at this little party tonight?"

"The usual suspects," Darcie said.

"She didn't invite my ex from high school, did she?" If anyone ever asked Troy if he'd been in love before, he'd have to say yes. And it would have been with Daisy. He'd cared for her a great deal during their two-year relationship.

But Daisy had never been the right girl for him—a fact made very apparent when she faked a pregnancy when he'd been a freshman at the Naval Academy. Lucky for him, her math skills were a little off and she sucked at lying.

"She'll be there, but that's not who Mom has her sights on." Darcie twisted her body. "There's a new girl in town. A chef at the Boathouse who does some catering on the side."

"Down by the ferry dock to Whidbey?" Troy asked.

"She rents in the neighborhood that overlooks the docks. She's a nice girl," Darcie said. "Her name's Priela Sloane, and she's catering the party, so technically not attending."

"Interesting how that worked out," Troy said under his breath. "You better not be part of this setup."

"I wouldn't pawn you off on a woman I like." Darcie tilted her head. "No offense, brother dear. You might be sweet and the kind of man who gives out your last dollar, but you make for a shit boyfriend and whenever anyone asks me if I know any single men, I always answer with, *none that I'd fix my close friends up with.*"

"I have to agree with my wife on this one," Reid chimed in.

"I'm not sure if I should be grateful or offended. However, it's not like I don't tell the women I date what they are in for." Troy ran a hand across his hair. "I don't understand why this family is so obsessed with my love life. I liked it better when they were worried about your career choice."

Darcie smiled. "Oh, trust me. When you're not here, Mom finds all sorts of ways to needle me."

Reid nodded. "When Darcie took out her last charter, I got a phone call at least once a day, asking me why I let her do it. As if I had a say in it."

Darcie gave Reid a gentle love tap on the shoulder. "What are you talking about? You encouraged me to do it."

"That is true."

"Before I forget," Darcie said. "Zane is coming solo."

"Our cousin Zane?"

"Do you know anyone else by that name?" Darcie glanced over her shoulder and glared. "Anyway. His girlfriend dumped him and he's not in the best of moods. Mom's trying to fix him up too."

"Is he still working at Club Allure?" Troy asked.

"He sure is." Reid laughed. "I suggested to your sister that we check it out, but then she told me it was a sex club. I was floored."

"You'd be shocked at how many people are members that live in this town. It's not what you think," Troy said.

"Oh yes, it is, and my husband isn't going anywhere near that place."

Troy leaned back and closed his eyes. It was good to be home. "So, back to the party. How mad will Mom and Dad be if I insult Priela's cooking because that should be easy enough and then maybe she'll hate me."

"Unless you want Mom to be relentless while you're here, I'd find a way to smile, be nice, and just avoid," Darcie said.

Easier said than done.

Priela Sloane wished she'd turned this job down, especially with the way Mrs. Bowie went on and on about her son, the Navy fighter pilot. Not to mention the number of people who swarmed Darcie and Reid's humble home. She'd met some of them, but she had no idea who most were. She had wanted to branch out, meet more people. Because catering was her passion, not being a chef in a restaurant. But she wasn't in a position where she could quit her job. Not yet, anyway.

However, it had been Mrs. Bowie who introduced her to Crystal which had been a total blessing. Besides owning a bakery, the woman knew everyone, and that meant more introductions, not to mention putting business cards in her store.

But the truly best part was the fact that Priela wasn't a baker. She could put together a decent dessert, but if she needed something truly decadent, Crystal promised to help her out. It could be a match made in culinary heaven.

Priela set the oven and leaned against the counter, tapping her cell phone and pulling up a blog she had started following called *Create the Dew.* It had become her guilty pleasure and she enjoyed the young woman, finding Dixie Gaynor to be a fascinating person. Her perspective on life was unique and refreshing, but also a bit of an enigma.

The sound of the kitchen door swinging open startled her and she jumped.

A younger gentleman with long dark hair sauntered into the space carrying a case of champagne. "Oh. Hi. I'm Zane Pierce. I'm Troy's cousin." He set the case on the counter.

"Nice to meet you." She nodded. "Have you heard when your cousin will be arriving?"

"Sorry. I haven't heard." He unpacked the bottles and loaded half into the fridge and the other half into a large bucket of ice.

Ziggy Bowie barreled her way into the kitchen with a bottle of wine. "Oh, hey, Zane. I see my mom has put you to work."

"That's what favorite nephews are for." He kissed her cheek. "And I have an entire list, so I better get moving before your brother gets here." He turned and smiled. "See you around."

Priela nodded.

"You sure know how to put on a spread." Ziggy set the wine on the counter and smiled. "This place looks great, and everything smells wonderful."

"Thank you," Priela said. Of all the Bowies who lived in Seattle, she knew Ziggy the least, although she'd heard Mrs. Bowie talk about her constantly, as she did with all her children, but Priela had spent a little time with Jag and his wife Callie as well as Darcie and her husband Reid, who was technically throwing this little shindig. "I love your dress."

"I borrowed it from Callie." Ziggy worked as a producer for the local news, and from what Priela had heard from the woman's siblings, she focused solely on her career and nothing else. "I hope my brother gets here soon." She glanced at her watch. "I've got to get back to the office. We're working on a big story."

"Sounds exciting," Priela said.

"It is." Ziggy nodded. "You're going to love my brother. He's wicked cool. There's my mom. I'll see you later."

Whenever Priela talked with Ziggy, she ended up with whiplash, where with Darcie and Jag, they had seemed to learn how to slow down and smell the roses.

"Priela, where do you want these?" Leslie Crystal asked, holding a tray of deviled eggs. Leslie was one of Kyle and Jenna's twin daughters, and she and her sister had been working for Priela after school and on weekends when they didn't have too much homework. Both were sweet girls, but damn, Priela was glad that she wasn't a teenager anymore.

"Those can go on the table I set up over in the

family room." She glanced at her watch. "Don't put the shrimp out until they get here, though, okay?"

"Wait until you see this guy." Leslie smiled. "He's like really hot for an old guy."

"Hey. Who are you calling old?" Jag stepped into the kitchen. "And you're too young to be looking at boys."

Leslie rolled her eyes. "I'm fifteen. And I was talking about your little brother, who is way cuter than you."

Jag laughed. "I think you need glasses."

"I'm going to go put these down. Do you need anything else?" the girl asked.

"No. I'm good until cleanup. Thanks." Priela wiped her hands on her apron. "Does your brother coming home for a visit always cause such fanfare?"

"Nope," Jag said as he snagged a fried conch from one of the trays Priela was keeping hot on a warming platter. "But the last time he came home, it was only for a night. He wasn't able to attend Darcie and Reid's wedding, and this will be the first time he meets my daughter. Plus, two months ago, he was awarded the Distinguished Flying Cross medal. No small thing. He doesn't like to talk about it, and he'd be pissed if anyone mentioned that this was in celebration of that. My brother can be a cocky son of a bitch, but when it comes to certain things, he's quite humble."

Priela knew all too well what that medal was all about. Not only had she been raised in a Navy family, but she'd also spent four years at the Naval Academy herself and another four having the military pay for her culinary education. Both her father and brother had served. And her father had the exact same medal, though her brother had not received the honor. As a matter of fact, her brother's naval career had been tainted by betrayal because the Navy refused to give those who loved him the most the details surrounding his death. Instead, they let innuendoes and rumors destroy his reputation, leaving Priela and her parents heartbroken.

"But he's a real-life hero," Jag said.

His wife came up behind him, carrying their three-month-old little girl. "I need you to be my personal hero and change your daughter's smelly diaper."

"Whatever you say, dear." Jag blew a raspberry on Stephanie's cheek. She laughed and kicked her feet while grabbing her daddy's face. "Let's go clean you up so you're all pretty to meet your uncle Troy."

Priela had to admit, she enjoyed the Bowie family. All of them. Even their overprotective, meddling mother, who kept hinting at what a catch her Troy would be for any young woman.

Callie snagged a wineglass and filled it. She held it high. "Lord knows I need this."

"Long day?"

"My nanny's mother is sick, which means my nanny didn't work today. I'm on deadline, and my husband couldn't take the day off. I love my little girl, and being a mom is amazing, but trying to write with a three-month-old underfoot is insane."

"I was busy cooking all day, but if I'm not working and you need help, feel free to call me. I love babies." And that was no lie. Priela was two birthdays shy of turning thirty, and while her biological clock hadn't started ticking yet, she could feel it getting wound up in her belly, reminding her that she wasn't getting any younger.

"Seriously?"

"I never offer myself up if I don't mean it."

"You might regret that because my nanny is going to be out for the next couple of weeks. I don't need someone every day since we have a lot of family who can help out, but they are all busy, too."

"Just tell me the days you need, and I'll let you know if I'm free."

Callie took a large gulp. "You're a lifesaver. I can't thank you enough. And I'll pay you what I pay my girl. I've been told we pay her pretty well."

"I'm sure it's fair."

The oven timer dinged. Priela turned, shutting it off and setting it to warm. "Any idea on when they will be here?"

"I got a text from Darcie that Troy landed about fifteen minutes ago. So, I'd guess they should be here in less than ten." Callie leaned forward. "Has my mother-in-law been really pushy?"

"About what?"

"Troy," Callie said matter-of-factly. "Or haven't you noticed there are a few single women at this party. I'm waiting for the music for the *Dating Game* to play."

"I thought everyone here was family or a close family friend." When Darcie and her mom had first approached Priela to cater the party, it had been presented as a small surprise gathering. But later, when Henrietta called with more details, the party had morphed into something entirely different. Not that she minded. The bigger the party, the more money she made. And boy, did she need it.

"For the most part, that is true, but Henrietta tossed in a few townspeople for good measure." Callie took a celery stick and nibbled. "For example, she invited the Hillfords and the Nagals. Both families lived in the neighborhood that Troy grew up in. The Nagal boys went to school with Troy, and they played sports together, but neither one lives in the area. Just their sister, Teresa, who happens to be single. And she and Troy never liked each other in school."

"Do they like each other now?" Priela asked, wondering why she found herself so fascinated by a man she'd never met, especially since he was in the Navy, meaning he was someone she had no interest in getting to know.

"I think they had a thing for about five seconds a year ago, but it didn't end well," Callie said, waving her veggie. "But then there is Daisy Hillford, Troy's high school sweetheart. She's a piece of work, but he's never been honest with his parents about why they broke up, so Henrietta keeps inviting her places, and Daisy keeps trying to sink her nasty little hooks into Troy."

"What did she do?" Crap. That was rude. "I'm sorry. I shouldn't have asked you that."

"No. It's fine, but it's too ugly to repeat, and

Troy doesn't know I know, and blah, blah, blah. Family dynamics are a pain in the ass sometimes." Callie polished off her vegetable and licked her fingers. "And, of course, there is you."

Priela waved her hands and took a step back. "I have a couple of hard and fast rules about dating. One of them is that I never go out with anyone in the military."

Callie arched a brow. "Really? Why not? If you don't mind me asking."

Priela didn't mind, but she wouldn't be truthful —not completely, anyway. "My dad was a career Navy man. He only retired a couple of years ago. The longest I lived anywhere was three years, and while I will admit that I got to see some awesome places, it's a hard life and not one I want to be in a relationship with."

"Well, that's good, then I don't need to warn you off. Because that's what I came over here to do and why I sent my husband off on diaper duty."

"Do you always cock-block your relatives?" Shit. Priela would get herself in a shitload of trouble if she didn't put a sock in it. "I didn't mean it that way."

"Yes, you did." Callie laughed. "I love Troy. He's an amazing man and a true hero. I wish he was different when it came to women, but between what happened with Daisy and my theory on his fear of having a family of his own, he never ends up lasting more than three months with any girl."

"My dad knew a couple of guys like that." Priela decided not to go digging into the whole Daisy thing. She didn't need to know. She was going to do her best to stay in the background, serve the food, restock trays, and clean. "He always sized them up and decided that some people were just better off that way."

Callie blew out a puff of air. "I agree, only Troy isn't one of those men. He's made for being the other half of a couple, and I know he'd make a great dad. Only for someone who says he's not afraid of anything, he's terrified of not being in control. Being in love and in a committed relationship takes that feeling away from him, and he doesn't know what to do."

"Or maybe marriage just isn't his thing." Priela had always been known for saying exactly what was on her mind, and it generally got her into a bit of trouble. "I don't know him, so I'm probably speaking out of turn. I just know a few people who don't want to ever get married, and they get tired of people telling them they will change their minds."

"I tend to agree with you." Callie stood tall, folding one arm across her midsection while holding up her glass of wine.

The family room behind her filled with more people. The background chatter blended with soft country music.

"But you're wrong about Troy, and I'll bet you one hour of free babysitting that after you meet him tonight, you'll agree with my assessment."

"And if I disagree, you have to pay me double for that hour."

Callie stretched out her hand. "But you have to promise me to be completely honest."

"I think I've proven in this conversation that I have a problem restraining my tongue."

"That's why I like you." Callie glanced at her Apple Watch. "They're here."

Wonderful.

Priela's heart beat against her rib cage, increasing in pressure and building in excitement. A man in the Navy shouldn't have this effect on her, no matter how intriguing.

So far, the evening had been a lot more fun than Troy had expected, though it was only an hour in. As long as he continued avoiding Daisy, life would be good. While it appeared she'd changed, he'd never trust her again. Hell, he didn't trust most members of the opposite sex. Not with his heart, anyway.

"Hey, cousin." Zane slapped him on the back. "It's good to see you and I hear you're here for more than one night."

Troy clinked his beer against Zane's. "What's shaken?"

"Not much."

"How's Club Allure?" Troy asked.

Zane checked his watched. "I've got to head

there now. Let's get together and have a drink while you're in town."

"Absolutely." Troy shook his cousin's hand and stared out into the sea of people. This was a night to celebrate him and that made him uncomfortable in his own skin.

A woman with her blond hair pulled back in a bun at the nape of her neck strolled by, carrying a tray of various seafood. She wore a formfitting white ribbed shirt that went all the way to her neck. Her dark slacks hugged her hips and thighs until they flared out on her lower legs.

She was slender and tall.

He sucked in a deep breath. His lungs burned. His vision blurred. He thought he might topple as he did his best to steady himself. Women affected him on all sorts of levels. He wasn't immune to attraction.

Just love.

"You like what you see?" Jag asked.

"Whoever she is, she's a knockout." She also walked as though she'd spent some time in the military. That was a swagger you didn't lose overnight. If ever. And on whoever that sexy number was, it only made Troy want to lift her into his arms and carry her to the nearest bed, strip her naked, and do all sorts of unspeakable things to her body.

His muscles tightened. He blew out a puff of air and did his best to think about anything but sex.

It had been a few months. He'd go find himself a hot little number tomorrow night, someone who didn't have crazy eyes and wouldn't want anything other than a short-lived sexual encounter.

"That's Priela. You know, one of the girls Mom wants to fix you up with."

"Well, that just took the wind out of my sails." Troy lifted his beer to his lips. No way would he get involved with anyone his family tried to set him up with. That always ended badly.

"I can't tell if Mom's trying to make Daisy jealous or Priela."

"I wish Mom would drop the whole Daisy thing. That woman is a loon," Troy said.

"Maybe if you told Mom what really happened, she'd respect that."

Troy wished he could, but he'd made a promise to Daisy's mother that he wouldn't, and Troy was nothing without his honor. Besides, Daisy came to these things, and then she left. For the most part, she stayed out of his way, though the last couple of times she did end up texting him later, wondering if they could be friends.

That wasn't a good sign.

"No. And don't make me regret telling you."

"I wouldn't break your confidence," Jag said, waving across the room to his wife, who had a fussy baby on her hands. "I'd better go see if I can help before I end up sleeping on the sofa tonight."

"No worries. I'm going to get some air," Troy said.

"I'll go with you." Kyle rounded the corner from the dining room into the family room.

Troy stepped out into the backyard and stared at the cloud-filled sky.

"It's good to see you," Kyle said. A few other people milled about in the yard, playing cornhole since it was unseasonably warm and wasn't raining.

"I was sorry to hear about your buddy down in Jupiter, Florida," Troy said.

"Yeah, that was a major shit show. It won't bring back my friend, but a year later, we got justice." Kyle sat at the table, putting a tray of delightful little meatball things that Darcie's caterer had made in front of them. Priela certainly knew her way around the kitchen, and she was gorgeous, too. Still, he'd yet to have a conversation with her, and considering where his mind kept going, he wasn't sure if he should.

If he spent any amount of time talking with Priela, his mother would be all up in his face, telling him to take her out and show the new girl around town. And then he'd have to say yes, because his mother had raised him right.

And while he'd only caught a glimpse of her, he was already intrigued, and that was never good when it came to him and women.

"What do you know about this Priela chick?" The moment the words rolled off his tongue, he wished he could take them back. He sipped his beer as he leaned against the railing. His little sister and Reid had bought a nice little cottage-style house not far from Jag and Callie in the small town of Langley. As kids, they'd all loved traveling on the ferry to Whidbey Island—or any of the islands, for that matter. But there was always something a little magical about this particular little seaside town and the way it overlooked Puget Sound.

Kyle laughed. "I know very little other than the fact that my girls love her, and she's given them some part-time work. What I do know, though, I like." Kyle cleared his throat. "But she keeps to herself, and I can't help but think there's a reason for that."

"She carries herself like she's had training."

"Her dad was a Navy guy. But like I said, she keeps to herself, and I respect that," Kyle said, waving to one of his kids. "Hey, bring me some of those."

Lilia stepped outside and set a tray down on the table.

"Are you having fun?" Kyle asked.

"Beats staying at home and doing homework." Lilia smiled. "And I have to stay to help clean up."

"Not a problem. Mom already told me we're waiting for you to be done."

"Thanks. She's paying us extra." Lilia kissed Kyle on the cheek. "I'd better get back to work. "Mrs. Bowie wants Priela to meet Troy." Lilia rolled her eyes. "If you ever try to fix me up—"

"You'll never have to worry about that," Kyle said with a gruff voice. "No one will ever be good enough."

Lilia disappeared into the house.

"I can't believe your girls are fifteen. They're both so grown-up," Troy said.

"Tell me about it. It's all I can do to keep the

boys away, and Jenna is constantly telling me I'm way overprotective."

"I would be, too," Troy admitted. "But they seem like good girls."

"Oh. They are. It's not them I'm worried about." Kyle ran a hand over his head. "And Michael is growing up way too fast."

"I couldn't believe how big Stephanie was. I expected her to be this tiny little thing, but she's already got a huge personality."

"She's a cutie." Kyle stabbed a meatball with a toothpick and stuffed it into his mouth.

"Can I ask you a question?" Troy had known Kyle for a long time. He was a lot older, but considering that Kyle was a retired Navy SEAL, he'd been a key player in helping Troy get into the academy, as well as navigating his career in the Navy.

"You know you can ask me anything."

"It's not like you to back anyone or anything, especially if your family is involved. Why wouldn't you pry or at least ask about Priela's past?"

"I didn't say I didn't ask anything about her. I just said I respect her privacy."

Troy arched a brow. "That's a very different statement."

"Indeed, it is."

"So, what do you know?"

"And why are you so interested?" Kyle cocked his head. His tone was more teasing than anything, but there was a protective undertone as if to say that this girl was off-limits for a one-night stand.

"You mean besides my family playing matchmaker?"

"Fair enough," Kyle said. "She went—"

"There you are." Troy's mother's voice tickled his ears. He glanced toward the sliding doors and bit down on his tongue when he saw Darcie's caterer standing next to his mother. And before Kyle had had a chance to fill him in on any details that might help him navigate the upcoming conversation.

Let the games begin.

"I've been looking all over for you," his mother said.

"I need to go find my wife." Kyle stood and gave him a good shoulder squeeze. "Good luck," he said with a smirk.

Time to play nice with his mother and the new girl.

He leaned in and kissed his mom's cheek. "I needed a breath of fresh air and to get away from the crowd."

"I know. We bombarded you on your first night, but if we didn't, this never would have happened." His mother grabbed his face and pinched. "Have you met Priela? She's the brilliant woman who cooked all this food today. She's so amazing."

"I have not had the pleasure." He set his beer on the table before extending his arm. She rested her fingers in his hand, and he raised it, pressing his lips to her soft, warm skin. "Your food is spectacular. I can't stop eating, though I've been full for like the last half hour."

"Thank you." She tugged her hand and clasped them behind her back. "That's the best compliment a chef can hear."

"Oh. Excuse me," his mother said. "I need to go chat with someone. You two have a seat and get to know each other. This poor girl hasn't had a break all night."

"I really should—"

"Take a break," his mother interrupted Priela.

He leaned in. "I'd do what she says," he whispered. "Or she'll just keep doing this until we sit down and spend a few minutes together." He offered her a chair and smiled.

She did not return the sentiment, and he certainly understood her reservations. His mother was never subtle while on the dating game rampage. Normally, Troy wouldn't engage by being so gentlemanly, but after talking with his family and friends, he wanted to humor his mother at least.

"I meant what I said about your chef skills, and not just because I've been stuck at sea, eating shit on a shingle for the last six months."

She cracked a smile. "I love creamed chipped beef on toast. I don't make it often, but I do it better than anyone I know."

"You can't be serious."

"Oh. But I can. I grew up on that meal," she said. "Whenever I get a little homesick, I make it."

"Where are you from?"

She took a toothpick and poked at one of the little meatball treats at the center of the table. "I never know how to answer that question because I've never lived in one place for more than a few years—except for in college."

He narrowed his stare. More and more women went to the Naval Academy. To be exact, about twenty-five percent of enrollment was women. So, if what he suspected was true, even if they had been there at the same time, their paths may have never crossed.

His pulse increased, though he wasn't sure if it was because his body was becoming increasingly aware of the sexy woman nibbling on a meatball and he wanted to feel her plump lips curling over all sorts of things…

Or the fact that he found himself wanting to know things about Priela.

A concept that made him uncomfortable. He only enjoyed knowing the women he was attracted to on a superficial level. He didn't let them get too close, and he never allowed himself to find out what made them tick.

The moment he laid eyes on Priela, he'd wanted her between the sheets.

Sitting with her here, now, he wanted to know her mind.

And that was a dangerous combination.

"What's the one place you've lived that felt like home?"

"To be honest, Seattle."

"That's interesting. I heard you've only lived here for a few months."

"But it's the first place I chose," she said. "I moved all around the world with my parents. They even picked where I went to school. When I graduated college, other than wanting to go to culinary school, the Navy owned my ass for the next four years."

His jaw slackened. While he'd suspected that to be true, he hadn't expected her to be so open about it. For some odd reason, he'd thought he would have to pull that information out of her as if he were an interrogator, and she, his prisoner.

Fuck.

Why the hell did that turn him on?

"Surprise you?"

"No. I actually suspected it by the way you walk, but I honestly didn't think you'd tell me. I don't know why."

"Perhaps it's because I also have a look of disdain." She waved her index finger around her face. "I mean no disrespect to you or to my father, who served until two years ago, but I never wanted to be in the service. I just wasn't given a choice."

"Last time I checked, our military was volunteer only."

"Not if you're a Sloane. Then it's a family duty, and you don't have a choice—or at least I didn't feel like I did. Unlike my brother, who couldn't wait to go to the academy and serve his country." She folded her arms across her chest.

A sudden chill rolled across Troy's skin. He'd

seen this anger against the military before, and he never took it personally.

His heart dropped to the pit of his stomach like a diver racing to the depths of the ocean. His pulse increased. He waited for his skin to break out in a cold sweat.

"Where's your brother now?"

"He's dead."

"Shit. I'm sorry for your loss." Troy ran a hand over his mouth. No wonder Kyle hadn't pried. Of course, now Troy wanted—*needed*—to know the circumstances around her brother's death. That kind of anger didn't come from a man's honorable passing. It came from unanswered questions. Or shame. He'd seen it a dozen times. His job was dangerous, and no matter how many times they vowed to watch their brothers' and sisters' backs, good men and women died in combat, as well as in training exercises.

"So am I."

"Did he die while on duty?" He knew he probably shouldn't ask. At least, not now, at his party. But he couldn't help himself. He genuinely wanted to know what put such sadness in her sweet light-blue eyes.

"You know what's funny?"

He shook his head, not finding anything about this conversation humorous.

"He was a fighter pilot, just like you."

Troy rubbed a hand over his freshly shaven face. "When was he killed?" He changed his choice of words.

"Two years ago. Three days before my last day of service."

"So, you had no intention of re-enlisting before your brother passed?"

"No. The military was never for me. I didn't want it, and I fought going to the Naval Academy at all, but my father wouldn't have paid for a regular college, and he was able to work out culinary school in my four years after school, so I figured eight years out of my life wouldn't be the worst."

Troy wanted to ask if she'd enjoyed her time but would save that for another discussion. "What happened to your brother?"

"I honestly don't know. They told me his plane went down in the Mediterranean." She raised her hands and slapped them on her thighs. "I asked your friend Kyle to help me, but he hasn't been able to get me anything."

"Help you with what, exactly?"

"To find out the truth behind my brother's death."

Troy scratched his neck. "You don't believe what they told you?"

"It was a top-secret mission, so the Navy keeps saying they can't give me a lot of details. What they have told my family and me is bullshit, and they all but blamed my brother for what happened. So, instead of giving him a medal, like you, they smeared his name. As a matter of fact, just a few months ago, they came out with what they are saying is their final report."

"And what did it say?" Troy wasn't sure he wanted to hear this. Very few investigations made national news, and the ones that did were never good. If this was one of those, he knew which one, and it was the worst kind.

"It said that my brother caused the incident that killed him. That he made a fatal error in judgment, which resulted in a tragic accident. But they can't explain how no one else in his squadron died that day, and none of them will talk to me. The one person I actually got on the phone said it was a miracle they got out alive but wouldn't elaborate and agreed with the Navy's statement about Isaac. It makes no sense."

Isaac Sloane.

Operation Pins and Needles.

Shit. Troy knew more about that mission than he ever wanted to admit, especially to Priela. But the bigger problem was that there were still so many questions, and the Navy had tasked him with studying the dogfight, which was only one very small piece of the puzzle. His squadron had come in after Isaac's plane went down and the conflict was coming to an end. But Troy would never forget it. It could be years before the Navy found out what really went down that day, but for the sake of peace, they'd placed the blame on themselves and gave the world a scapegoat.

The government had been left with no choice, especially since the enemy wasn't being cooperative, and Isaac *had* made a pivotal mistake. One that forced the Navy's hand. One they couldn't deny.

The history books would forever tell the story that Isaac and the rest of his flyboys broke the rules of engagement, which cost Isaac his life. It was the only narrative the Navy could tell that wouldn't start a war with a hostile country that had terrorist cells ready to launch on US soil.

Sometimes Troy hated his current security clearance with his new position with Delta Force and the Special Tactics Squadron. He loved his career, and he loved flying, but the secrets made for some killer heartburn.

"You served, you know the military isn't perfect, and there are reasons why they might not be able to give you—"

"You sound like my father, Kyle, and every other person I know in the Navy. I don't need excuses. I need answers, and the world needs to know the truth. Do you have any idea what it's like to have your brother, a man who loved his country, be accused of nearly causing a war because he was being cocky? That all he wanted to do was show off his skills in front of some foreign fighter pilot asshole?"

No. But neither of them had all the facts. And even with his security clearance and current knowledge of the situation, his hands were tied. He wasn't at liberty to say one fucking word on the subject.

And even if he knew what'd really happened that day, he still couldn't tell Priela. Not unless he wanted to risk his career—something he'd never do. Not for anyone.

She stood, gracefully smoothing down the front of her slacks. "I apologize for how I just behaved.

Thank you for your service. I need to get back to work. This is a paying gig for me."

He stood. "No need to apologize to me." He took her shoulder and squeezed. "If you ever want to talk, let me know."

"I appreciate it, but that's unlikely." She stepped around him and waltzed into the family room, zigzagging through the crowd.

Damn. He pulled out his cell and texted Kyle.

Troy: *How much do you really know about Isaac Sloane?*

Kyle: *Probably less than you.*

Troy: *That doesn't answer my question.*

Kyle: *Very little, other than she's never going to get the answer she's looking for. Isaac engaged the enemy. He did start that dogfight. And it ended badly.*

Troy: *That sounds like you know something.*

Kyle: *I know people who were there. One of them is on the other end of this text message.*

Troy had only witnessed the end of the dogfight. By the time he got there, the enemy was bugging out. Since then, he'd been forced to go over that day's events a million times, and each time, he came up with the same result.

Isaac got fucked.

Kyle: *She's angry at the Navy. And she's mad at her*

father for defending the institution. She believes everyone is allowing her brother to be the fall guy.

Troy: *We both know that's the truth.*

Kyle: *Doesn't matter what we think we know. Or what we've experienced in our lifetimes. We do the things we do because, at the end of the day, even if the world doesn't understand, we do. The Navy is right on this. You know it, and so do I.*

Troy: *She and her father were still enlisted when her brother died.*

Kyle: *She'd already gotten her walking papers, and neither of them had the clearance to be briefed on the subject. You need to let this one go. I have.*

Somehow, Troy doubted that, and there was no way in hell he would let her walk around with that kind of rage eating at her soul. It would destroy her, and he had the power to ease her pain.

He just had to find the right way to approach the situation without getting himself into trouble or giving her too much information. She needed just enough to know that while her brother had made a mistake, he'd also saved lives.

Priela stood on her deck that overlooked the ferry dock that connected the mainland to Whidbey Island. She'd picked the area in part because it was far enough away from the city, yet close enough that catering jobs there wouldn't be a hassle. But the real reason was the call to the water and the sky.

She had to admit there was nothing more beautiful than the way any body of water met the sky at the horizon. It was as if they were destined to touch, like long-lost lovers.

The only thing she hadn't thought about was the long line of cars that would park outside her home, waiting for the ferry. And not just once a day… multiple times. It got annoying. She glanced at her watch. Her heart lurched to the back of her throat. She tried to swallow but couldn't.

She'd been so wrong about how she'd treated Troy last night, and she owed him one hell of an apology. Just because he was in the Navy didn't mean he knew anything or could find out what really happened to her brother. She understood the way things worked, but she didn't have to like it, and she would continue creating a stink until someone listened.

And then there was the immediate attraction she'd had for Troy. And not the kind of head-turning where you saw someone across the room, thought they were cute, and considered striking up a conversation later in the night. But the kind of sexual desire that made women go weak in the knees. When she first laid eyes on him, Priela had thought her heart might pound right out of her chest, she became so excited. Every erogenous zone had nearly exploded. It'd taken all her energy to keep her mind focused on the task at hand.

Turning, she strolled inside and snagged her keys. She'd asked Troy to meet her at the coffee shop on Whidbey Island right at the ferry terminal. She figured she'd walk on the boat, take a nice ride across Puget Sound, snag a great cup of Joe, say what she needed to, and then head back home. Other than having to save face, it wouldn't be a horrible way to spend a couple of hours.

She had to admit, though, if only to herself, that she had loved her time on a battleship. Being on the water had always been calming to her. As she locked the front door and double-timed it toward the approaching ferry, a helicopter buzzed over-head. She'd always enjoyed being transported anywhere via bird. She often resented how much she'd actually liked her time in the Navy, when all she wanted was to hate the institution for shitting on her brother's memory as if his life—that he'd given for his country—didn't matter.

Pulling the zipper of her fleece all the way up to her chin, she shivered. A cold rush of salty hair smacked her face the second she stepped onto the top deck of the boat. She stuffed her hands into her pockets and stared across the Sound. Fog lifted off the water as if it were sailing toward the sky, meeting the clouds that hovered low with moisture, threatening to release a slight drizzle. All her friends in San Diego, where her folks had retired, thought she was insane to move to rainy Seattle. But she loved it.

The ferry pushed from the dock and headed out

into the Sound toward Whidbey Island. She rode the ferry at times just to be out in the open air and on the water. Perhaps when she'd saved enough money, she'd buy a small boat. For now, she might take Darcie up on her offer to go for a nice sail with her and her husband.

Whidbey had to be her favorite island in the area, though they were all great, and she loved exploring each of them. Every time she went, she found a new trail or a little piece of history to learn about. Even when she went back a second time, she experienced it differently.

She headed down the stairs and stood in the long line of people as the ferry docked. Troy had thought it odd that she wanted to meet at a coffee shop at the docks and not at a restaurant or even at his sister's house, but he'd agreed with little hesitation, and quite graciously.

She strolled down the pavement with her mouth watering. Oddly, this little seaside diner had the best coffee. Too bad they didn't have Crystal's baked goods. That would round off the morning.

Stepping up to the outdoor counter, Priela pulled out a few dollars. "Two extra-large, please." She could smell the bitter flavor. It hit the back of her throat, making her stomach jump with excitement long before she even held the paper mug in her greedy little hands. "Thank you." She stuffed the change into her pocket, snagged a couple of sugar packets and cream, and found an outdoor table facing the parking lot. It wasn't horribly cold out, especially since the wind had died down and the sun was trying to burn through the clouds. Spring was certainly in the air.

The sound of a powerful motorcycle engine caught her attention. She glanced up and bit back a smile.

Nothing sexier than a man on a Harley.

Or one who obviously enjoyed his vacation days and didn't shave.

Troy flipped the kickstand and eased the bike to its side before shutting down the engine. "Good morning."

"Perfect timing." She held up one of the coffees. "Nice and fresh."

He pulled out a bag from the back satchel on the Harley. "That will go perfectly with some of Crystal's breakfast pastries."

"No way. Where on earth did you get those?" She tried not to stare into his dark-chocolate eyes. Her physical attraction to him needed to be sidelined.

"She left a bunch at Darcie's last night just for me, and even though some might disagree, I am a nice guy."

"That's a great lead-in to why I wanted to talk to you this morning." Might as well start the conversation right. "I'm sorry if I made you uncomfortable last night. I didn't mean to offend you."

He opened the bag filled with all sorts of decadent treats, offering them to her. She couldn't refuse.

She reached in and took a glazed apple fritter. It was still warm as if he had pulled it right from the oven, and it smelled like she'd just stepped onto an apple farm.

"Honestly, you didn't." He took the top off his coffee and dumped in one creamer and some sugar. He gave it a quick stir before bringing it to his lips. "I can certainly understand your frustration."

"Whether you understand it or not, I had no right to say the things I did, especially on your special night. And for that, I'm truly sorry." She kept her voice steady and strong.

"Apology accepted." He flipped the chair and straddled it. "I meant what I said. If you ever want to talk about things, I'm happy to lend an ear."

She pulled off a chunk of her pastry and

plopped it into her mouth. "If I start talking, I'll probably end up having to say I'm sorry again."

He blew into his coffee, staring intently as if he were searching for an answer. Or maybe a question. "How old are you?"

She jerked her head back. "That's an odd question."

He lifted his gaze. "I'm thirty. Well, closer to thirty-one, but I'm guessing you're a couple of years younger than me."

"I'm twenty-eight."

"That means we went to the Naval Academy at the same time."

"Well, now, that's interesting. Because so did my brother, but he would have turned thirty-three this year."

"So, he would have graduated two years before me."

"Did you know him? Isaac Sloane," she said with a little more excitement than she liked. She'd never crossed paths with Troy—that she knew of, anyway—so what made her think her brother had?

"I racked my brain last night thinking about both of you, and I don't think so. It would have made more sense that I would have recognized you, considering the lower percentage of women at the academy. But believe it or not, I was so focused on my studies that I didn't have much of a social life."

"I find it hard to believe that a good-looking guy like you was a nerd."

He chuckled. "I'm a bit of a type A personality. And from the time I was five years old, all I wanted to do was fly a fighter jet for the Navy. Everything I did was a means to reach that goal."

"Now that you have, what's next?" she asked.

"This feels weird to say out loud, but I was recently requited to Delta Force."

"Not many SEALs go that way. It's more of an Army thing." Her heart jumped to the back of her throat. "Doesn't that come with a pretty high security clearance?"

He nodded. "But you know as well as I do that doesn't mean I can go asking for information about a mission that has nothing to do with me, especially when they've given their final report."

She blew out a long breath. There was no reason for her to be angry with Troy. He'd done nothing to her personally. His professional organization sucked. What bothered her about Troy, her father, and other men and women in their positions was that they fed the beast. They believed it was okay for the military to lie for the sake of so-called national security.

Well, she called that bullshit.

Her brother deserved better.

"Their report is bullshit. And if you read it, you'll agree."

"I plan on taking a good look at it this after-noon," he said.

She dropped her pastry onto her lap. "Shit." She scooped up the sticky apple filling with a napkin. "Why?"

"I heard what happened," he said. "Every flyboy has. And we all know the statement, but I haven't read the report." His gaze shifted up and to the left.

Recalling her psychology classes, she thought that when someone did that with their eyes, specifi-cally in that direction, it meant that they were lying. But what did she know about a person's body language? She was a chef. About the only thing she could read was pleasant or disgusted facial expres-sions regarding her cooking.

Thankfully, she rarely saw the latter these days.

"That still doesn't tell me why you'd want to read the Navy's official report."

"I'm curious. There are a lot of questions about

what happened. Maybe I can read between the lines."

"So, you think you can interpret better than I can?" Anger flowed through her veins like an out-of-control wildfire. Every time this topic came up, she had no control over her emotions. It was one of the reasons she'd moved from San Diego, where she'd lived only a few blocks from her parents, and settled in Seattle. She'd never expected to run into so many Navy boys who would trigger these reactions. "The more you and I hang out, the more I'm going to need to apologize."

"It's not necessary. Really. I get it."

"I don't think you do." She wiped her fingers on a napkin. "You haven't lost a sibling or had someone smear their reputation."

"I've seen the government and the military do some pretty strange things. And while I will admit to loving my career and saying that I wouldn't give it up, I do know there are some flaws, and the institution needs some major changes." He held up his hand when she opened her mouth. "I want to know what you believe happened. You must have a theory."

She pinched the bridge of her nose. She'd thought about this so many times. Her brother could be a cocky son of a bitch, but what fighter pilot wasn't? If he wasn't living on the edge, pushing his body and his mind to the limits, he thought he might as well be dead. He also tended to believe that he was right, and when challenged, could become obnoxious while proving his correctness.

"The only thing I know for sure is that no one actually saw that dogfight in the sky, but there is no way my brother started it. He would never break the rules of engagement. And while the report specifically states that he did not receive permission to fire, he was being fired at, and that means the enemy engaged first."

"There is footage of what happened."

"And it shows Isaac being forced into enemy airspace." She downed the last bit of her coffee, which was still warm, but she wished it had been hot so she could feel the burn. "And it sounds like you've already read the report."

"I might have skimmed it." He knocked his knuckles on the table. "I want to help you, but you have to understand that the answers you're searching for might not be the ones you want."

"I could live with that if I was being told the truth."

He nodded. "Give me a couple of days to do some research. I'll see what I can find out."

"You'd do that for me?"

He held up his finger. "On one condition."

"I'm afraid to ask."

"Take a ride with me," he said.

"What. Now?"

"Yes. Let's go up to Fort Casey. I love it there. And the sun is coming out. It would be fun. Come on. What do you say?" He smiled wide and winked. "And for the record, I'll look into your brother regardless."

She laughed. "That doesn't ease the pressure on hanging out with you for the afternoon to get what I want."

He raised his palms to the sky. "Outside of your obvious anger issues with my profession and the military, I find you fascinating, and I want to get to know you."

She cocked her head. Single sailors on leave generally wanted two things: to let loose and get laid. She suspected that Troy had that attitude, and she wasn't going to be a notch on his bedpost. She wasn't that girl. She had too much respect for herself and, frankly, for him.

He rolled his eyes as if he knew exactly what she

was thinking. "I'm being serious. You're pretty cool, and from what my sister says, you have the same fascination with lighthouses as I do."

"Your sister has a big mouth."

"Darcie actually doesn't. But my other sister, Ziggy, well… that's a different story entirely. Come on, what do you say? Let's go up to Fort Casey and check out the lighthouse."

"Haven't you seen it like a million times?"

He nodded. "But it's a beautiful day, and the sun is shining. How often does that happen here?"

Why was she even entertaining this? She'd taken the ferry by foot because she'd planned to hop right back on the next one and head back to the mainland.

"Did you have plans today?" he asked.

She shook her head.

"Then what do you have to lose?"

He had a point, and she did miss riding on the back of a motorcycle. "You've got a deal, but you also have to throw in a late lunch at that pizza place in Langley."

He stood, holding his stomach. "That pizza is almost as good as the little ones you made last night."

"Flattery won't get you anywhere with me." She

took his hand and inched closer, her heart in her throat.

"It got me a smile."

Her cheeks heated. If he weren't in the Navy, she'd kiss him. But he was, and she had no room for a man in her life anyway. "Let's go before I change my mind." Or before she grabbed him in the parking lot and did things she shouldn't.

Troy usually thought of himself as a decent man, but he didn't have much self-respect right now. Lying didn't come easy, not even when necessary, and this game he was playing with Priela could backfire if he wasn't careful.

He'd never tell her all he knew. He couldn't. If he did, it would be the end of his career as he knew it—that was if anyone ever found out. The Navy had their reasons for closing the books on this one. He didn't completely understand it because his new commander had him studying the dogfight that'd led to Isaac's death. Did that mean his superiors believed something other than what was in the report? All Troy had been tasked to do was review the tactical maneuvers for future teaching purposes. It was standard procedure.

And he didn't even want to deal with what having Priela's arms wrapped around his middle did to the building sexual attraction he felt for the beautiful woman.

It wasn't just her looks that had gotten his attention. Her confidence had blown him away. Add in her intelligence, and it was a sweet recipe for the kind of disaster his father always told him would happen, and his mother wished for daily.

When she'd called, asking to meet for coffee, he almost hadn't agreed, simply because he knew he would end up asking her to go for a ride. He'd honestly been surprised that she had agreed.

He pulled into the parking lot at Fort Casey and eased down the bumpy road, avoiding a few potholes. He parked at the end of the line of cars, completely impressed with how she understood to use her body as he leaned the motorcycle over on the kickstand. "I just need to get a pass before we go walking around."

"Sounds good." She swung her leg over and took his hand. "That was an awesome ride. I haven't been on a bike in a few years."

"Did you own one?" He pulled out two water

bottles from the back storage compartment and handed her one.

She shook her head. "An old boyfriend did, and he got me hooked. I just never felt comfortable driving one this size."

"She is a beast."

"Do you leave her here?"

"She belongs to Jag," Troy said. "He lets me have her whenever I'm home. That's his excuse for keeping it. Otherwise, I think Callie would make him sell it at this point." He placed his hand on the small of Priela's back and guided her toward the kiosk. "Not that she has a thing against bikes, but his job is dangerous enough, and with a baby, she'd rather he not push his luck."

"I think that's fair."

"I'd have to agree." Seeing his older brother with a baby in his arms had fundamentally changed Troy on some level. It hadn't made him want to have a family all of a sudden, but between little Stephanie and Darcie being pregnant, it filled Troy's heart with something he'd never experienced before: a deeper kind of love. And the depths of emotion he had for his siblings had always been his driving force. The mere thought of his parents and siblings had kept him company many nights while he sat somewhere in the dark, wondering if he'd make it out alive.

If he felt that much stronger for his niece, he couldn't imagine what it would feel like if he ever fell in love with a woman and had a child.

It would most definitely be disastrous to his career.

"I'm surprised you feel that way, considering what you do for a living." She tucked a piece of blond hair that had blown across her face behind an ear. Her bright eyes caught the sun and sparkled like brilliant diamonds.

It took his breath away.

"I can appreciate how true love can change people's perspective on life. Darcie's husband was an adrenaline junkie. I mean, a legit thrill seeker. Now that he's about to be a dad, I don't think you'd catch him jumping out of a perfectly good airplane, and he's done that probably more times than I have."

"I'd heard he was wild and crazy back in the day."

"That's putting it mildly," Troy said. "I wouldn't even consider some of the things he's done, but he made a living at it, and he's also a safety nut, so there is that." Troy let his arm drop from her back, snagging her hand. He knew it was a bold move and that he shouldn't do it. Even as he clasped his fingers around hers, he told himself to stop.

But his body just wouldn't follow his brain's command.

She glanced up at him with an arched brow, though she had a bit of a smile and didn't let go.

So, neither did he.

However, he wished he hadn't bothered with the waters because now he had to carry one in his other hand, and the need to twist off the cap and take a sip would inevitably tempt one of them to break their connection.

And that would be a bummer.

"Reid seems like a nice guy."

"He's a good man, and my sister loves him, so that's all that matters."

"You really care about your family," she said as if that were a rare commodity.

"That seems to surprise you."

"No. It's just that you all tend to bend over backward for one another. That doesn't happen a lot."

Troy led her to a spot in front of the water and took a seat on a grassy patch where they could enjoy the view. Sadly, it meant no more hand-holding, so he broke down and took a swig of his water, which he desperately needed. "I hate to bring up a sad subject for you, but were you not close with Isaac?"

An immediate sheen came across her eyes. "He was about five years older than me, so when he left for the academy, I was only in eighth grade. I was the pain-in-the-ass little sister whom he had to babysit all the time, and I was already throwing temper tantrums about having to join the Navy in order to go to college. He would get so frustrated with me that he would often storm off."

"You don't feel like you had any other choices?"

She shook her head. "My father told me after I did my time that I could do whatever I wanted and he'd support me. He followed through with that promise. What the Navy didn't pick up and pay for, he did."

"I'm sure your dad's a good man, but I don't agree with forcing anyone into the service."

"I always wanted to own my own business, so I wanted to get a degree in hospitality, restaurant management, or business, as well as go to culinary school. The Naval Academy did offer me something, but just not everything. My mother talked me into appeasing my dad with the idea that it wasn't very long, and I'd still be able to get everything I wanted in the end. I went in with the attitude that I'd get kicked out. I got a demerit on my second day."

"That's one way to do it." He picked up a blade of grass and fiddled with it. "Have you gotten everything you want?"

"I'm close," Priela said with a beaming smile. "I'm catering, which is all mine. And I work at a nice restaurant with a flexible schedule. When I make enough money on my own to quit that, I will open a full-time catering business and hire more than a couple of teenage girls."

"Why not a restaurant?"

"That's a possibility down the road, too, but I love catering. It's so personal, and I like that." She glanced up, staring at him with inquisitive eyes. "Can I ask you something?"

"Of course."

"What would you do if you weren't in the Navy?"

"I'd open my own flight school."

"Wow. You answered that fast," she said, jerking her head back. "Most career military men vow they will never leave and act all indignant if you ask."

"Well, my father always told me to have a

backup plan in case things went to shit. He drove that into us for our entire lives. When Darcie became a yachtie, he was beside himself because he worried that she didn't have anything to fall back on. Honestly, she didn't have a plan, but she's a smart girl, and she's figuring it out."

Priela waved her finger under his nose. "But you have a plan."

He tossed his head back and laughed. "Like hell, I do. I never plan on leaving the Navy. You simply asked what I'd do if I weren't in the Navy, and that's the answer I've been giving my dad for a decade. Unless I become incapacitated or someone tells me I can't do my job anymore for some reason, I can't imagine doing anything else."

"What about love? Marriage? A family?" she asked. "Where does that fit into your life?"

"It doesn't," he admitted. "A fact that breaks my mother's heart. And I do hate that, but I can't see myself being able to live my life this way with a wife and kids, especially now that I'm in Delta Force. It wouldn't be fair to them, and I guess I'm too selfish to give up my goals for someone else."

"I don't think that's selfish. I believe it's honest. I wouldn't give up my hopes and dreams for any man." She laid her hand on his knee and squeezed gently. "My mother followed my dad all over the globe, and she loved it. And I can't honestly sit here and say that I hated the lifestyle. I lived more in my first eighteen years than most do in their entire lifetime."

"But you resent the military."

"Not for my upbringing." She wiped a tear that'd escaped her eye. "And if I'm being frank, I received a top-notch education and learned and experienced things I wouldn't have had I not gone to the Naval Academy. But I think the military can do better by all their heroes."

Troy wished it were that simple.

"Imagine if it had been you up in the air that day, and it had been your plane that engaged the enemy and went down. How would your family feel about the Navy saying that it was your fault?"

He opened his mouth, but no words came out. His pulse increased. Not once had he thought about it in those terms. Jag would never believe that he'd make such a fatal error in judgment, and while Isaac had done what many skilled fighter pilots would have done, the fact remained: He'd crossed over into enemy airspace, and he didn't disengage after the opposition fired a warning shot.

And that was the big distinction.

"Did you know my brother received almost as many medals as you?" she asked.

"I did know that," he admitted. "I looked it up last night."

"Do you see why I don't believe what they're saying?"

"I do. And I get your point about what you said about my family." The more she talked, the more he wanted to tell her what he knew and didn't know. But not just yet.

He needed to spend some more time looking at the footage and reading all the reports. So far, it had only been an assignment to be used in flight schools —something that needed careful consideration when he returned from leave.

Well, instead of chasing tail for the next two weeks, he'd be working.

He could think of worse things.

"Let's go get some pizza." He jumped to his feet. "After that, I have some major reading to do tonight."

She stood, resting her hands on his shoulders. "Thank you. Most people brush me off as a crazy, bitchy sister."

"You kind of come off that way at first."

"I suppose I do." She tilted her head.

He shouldn't take that as an invitation, but he did. He leaned in and brushed his mouth over her sweet lips. When she didn't pull away—or worse, slap him—he deepened the kiss, drawing her closer, wrapping his arms around her slender waist, careful not to get too carried away with where he placed his hands. He was not trying to get Priela into bed. Not that the thought hadn't crossed his mind. But she was special and not the kind of girl anyone had a fling with.

So, why the hell was he kissing her?

"I'm sorry. I shouldn't have done that." He took a step back.

"And I probably shouldn't have participated." She licked her lips.

He groaned. "Come on." He took her by the hand. "I don't know about you, but I'm starving."

"Someone did promise to buy me a late lunch."

"That I did." Somehow, he'd have to get through the rest of the day without allowing his mouth anywhere near hers.

4

"Yᴏu don't have to take me to my door. I literally live across the street from the ferry docks." Priela reached for her wine and took a small sip. They had ordered a nice, crisp bottle of white that tasted like a cold pear. They'd been seated at a booth in the front of the restaurant, overlooking the Sound. The wind had picked up a little, and a few sailboats raced across the water as the sun settled into the horizon.

"Besides the fact that I want to, it's getting dark, and if my mother ever found out I didn't walk you home, she'd smack me upside the head and lecture me for an hour. I'd have no choice but to sit there and listen. And what's worse is she'd come knocking on your door to apologize on my behalf."

Priela covered her mouth and tried to stifle a giggle to no avail. "That's adorable."

"Not really."

"Your mother's sweet," she said.

"That I can get on board with." He held up the menu. "Have you decided on what kind of pizza you want?"

"I'm a simple girl. Meat and cheese."

"Sounds good to me." He glanced toward the front door. "Looks like we have company." He waved to his brother, Jag, and his family. "Let me see that little girl." He stood and yanked Stephanie from his brother's arms, immediately blowing raspberries on her cheek.

She giggled and kicked her little feet.

"What are you two doing here?" Troy moved over, making room for his brother, who wore his badge on his shirt, but Priela didn't notice a weapon.

Callie parked a stroller at the end of the booth and sat next to Priela. "Neither of us felt like cooking," Callie said.

"But there seems to be a twenty-minute wait for a table, and Stephanie won't wait that long, so we're glad we can join you." Jag rested his arm on the back of the bench.

"No one invited you." Troy continued making faces at Stephanie and kissing his niece's cheek as if she were the only person in the room.

It made Priela's heart turn to mush. Someday, she wanted to find the right man, settle down, and have a kid or two. She wasn't exactly sure how that would look, but she knew without a doubt that she wanted that kind of life. She didn't know what it would mean to be in one place, and she wasn't even sure she'd stay in Seattle for more than a year or two. Not because she didn't like it, because she did, but because she didn't know how to grow roots.

"You're the one who gestured us over." Jag laughed as he lifted the wine, pointing to it and signaling for the waitress to bring over two more glasses. "I'll buy a second bottle."

"Aren't you working?" Priela asked. "I mean, I noticed you still have your badge on."

"I'm off duty." He unclipped it and stuffed it into his pocket. "I meant to take that off and lock it up with my weapon, but I forgot."

"I didn't mean to sound judgmental," Priela said.

"No worries." Jag smiled. "It wouldn't be a good look to have the chief of police drinking on the clock, even though I'm kind of always on the job."

The waitress set two fresh glasses on the table. She also took an order for two medium pizzas, both loaded with meat.

"Seriously, I hope you don't mind, Priela." Jag reached for his daughter, and Troy almost didn't give her up. "I know we invaded your date, but if we had to wait for a table, we'd be dealing with a screaming baby and would be going home without dinner." He cradled Stephanie while his wife handed him a bottle.

"I wouldn't have expected the two of you to hook up. So, how did it happen?" Callie asked.

Troy cocked his head. "Nothing like being blunt."

"Have you ever known me to be anything else?" Callie shrugged.

Priela's cheeks heated. She cleared her throat. "I owed Troy an apology for something I said last night, so I offered to buy him a cup of coffee."

"How did that turn into pizza?" Jag asked. "And I hope he's buying. Otherwise, I might have to tell Mom on him."

"You know, she still thinks it was the neighbor who broke the window. I could tell her the truth."

"This razzing could go on all night," Callie leaned over and whispered. "I hope Troy's been behaving himself."

"We've had a nice day." Quickly, she changed the subject to something that wouldn't make *her* uncomfortable. "Your daughter is just too stinking cute."

"Remind me of that at three in the morning." Callie let out a long sigh. "She's teething, and it seems that it bothers her most in the middle of the night."

"My cousin always complains that as soon as she gets used to one schedule, her baby, who is now two, decides it's time to adjust to a new one." Priela couldn't stop glancing between Troy and Stephanie. There was a strong family resemblance, though she could see Callie in the baby's eyes.

"That sounds about right," Jag said. "So, what are you two doing after dinner?"

"I've got to get home," Priela interjected. She understood the teasing that went on between siblings, especially brothers who appeared to be as close as these two clearly were, but she didn't want to be at the center of it. "I have a busy day tomorrow catering a lunch, and then I'm working at the restaurant tomorrow night."

"Bummer. I was going to ask if you wanted to come out on the boat tomorrow with me, Darcie, and Reid," Troy said.

"That would have been nice. Maybe another time." Priela shouldn't have given him an open invitation to ask her out again. She needed to nip whatever was brewing between them in the bud. She'd been attracted to men before, and she didn't let them screw with her goals.

Not that Troy was getting in the way of her achieving her dreams. How could he when he was only in town for a couple of weeks? But in the last twenty-four hours, she'd found herself obsessing over him on two levels.

The first being that she wanted to know what it would be like to have him in her bed, if only once.

The second for the information that he might be able to give her regarding her brother's death.

The fact that she could be honest with herself about the order of things disturbed her because she'd been totally focused on her brother since he died. All her energy and emotion had been wrapped up in Isaac and not always in a good way.

"Since Darcie isn't taking out charters until after the baby's born, she and Reid do a lot of day trips. I'm sure we can find a time that will work for you while I'm here." Troy smiled as though he'd found a prize at the bottom of a cereal box.

"I feel bad that you're catering our party after the christening." Callie took Stephanie from her husband and lifted her over her shoulder to pat her back. "If we pay you a little more, can you hire another staff person to work the party so you can come as Troy's plus one?"

Unfortunately, she asked the question just as Priela took a sip of wine, and she nearly choked on it. Some dribbled out of her mouth and down her chin. She grabbed her napkin and wiped her lips.

"Callie, seriously? That's not cool," Troy said, shaking his head. "I apologize for my sister-in-law. It seems my family doesn't know when to quit."

"I should have said so you can come as our guest." Callie lowered her chin. "And I think Priela and I know each other well enough at this point that she knows I was just adding to all the banter."

"I do get it, and I appreciate the invite." She pounded her chest and swallowed. The Bowie family was intoxicating. Every single one of them had a genuine kindness about them that couldn't be faked. Even their mother, who could be a bit over-bearing at times. Still, she always meant well and had a heart of gold. "But I won't take any more money from you, and I love my job. I'm just honored you trusted me with all the details."

"You are the best in town," Jag said.

"Based on last night, I'd have to agree." Troy raised his wineglass. "And I'll be happy to stay late and help clean up."

"Oh. Because you were so helpful at Darcie's." Priela tilted her head and cracked a slight smile. Granted, she and Troy hadn't gotten off on the right foot, and she'd done her best to avoid him after that first encounter. And he'd pretty much stayed outside with his buddies.

"Ouch." He took his napkin and placed it on his lap while the waiter placed the two pizza pies on the table, along with all the plates.

Jag served his wife while she set the sleeping baby in the stroller.

The pizza smelled like meat heaven. A perfect blend of sausage and pepperoni drizzled in sauce and covered in sizzling cheese.

"For the record, I was a little intimidated by you." Troy placed a heaping slice in front of her. "And I wanted to learn more about your brother before I reached out. But you beat me to it."

Her tastebuds came alive as she folded the thin crust and brought it to her lips. Troy might've actually been wrong. This pie might be better than hers.

Stranger things had happened.

"Thanks again for your help with that," Priela said.

"It's my pleasure." He held her gaze for a long moment.

She couldn't break the connection. Not that she wanted to, but she knew she should. The longer she stayed in his company, the stronger the desire to know him became.

And that wasn't good. She knew exactly what kind of man she wanted as a partner in life, and she was staring at someone who fit that description.

Except for his career.

And a few other things. But her brain couldn't find those things currently.

Her heart hammered in her chest. Everything around her but Troy blurred into the background. If they were sitting next to each other, they would likely be kissing.

Stephanie let out a startled cry, making Priela jump.

Troy dropped his pizza in his lap. "Shit."

"She does that a lot during these short evening naps but then goes right back to sleep." Callie glanced at her watch. "She'll be up in about twenty minutes and be a holy terror until bedtime."

"I can't imagine she's ever anything but a little sweetheart." Troy snagged another napkin and continued cleaning up the mess he'd made.

"Take her for an entire night, and then you can make that judgment," Jag said.

"I'd be happy to," Troy said.

"Seriously?" Callie asked. "Because Jag's got a night off soon, and he's been promising to take me glamping."

"I'll come over for the night. I'm sure Darcie and Reid will be happy to get rid of me for an evening," Troy said.

Priela wished she didn't want to watch Troy spending time with his niece, but she did. She could actually picture the two of them together, and it was a beautiful sight.

"But won't Mom get upset? I know she loves taking care of Stephanie every chance she gets." Troy tossed his dirty napkin on the table.

"She does, but not for overnights. Not until she's sleeping through the night. And she's not doing that, so be forewarned that Stephanie can sometimes be up for an hour or more with this teething thing."

"I can handle it."

Priela laughed but quickly squelched it.

"You don't think I can do this?" Troy cocked his head.

"Oh. No." She held up her hand and shook her head. "I can tell you can handle a baby when she's all cute and cuddly. I'm just not sure you'd know what to do with one who's over-the-edge fussy. Or worse, inconsolably cranky."

"That's a good way to describe our little girl." Jag nodded to someone who waved as they passed. "So, you can say no. But if you say yes, I'm holding you to it. A night alone with my wife is long overdue."

"I can do anything for one night." Troy wiped his hands on his napkin and tossed it onto his plate.

"I kind of want a ticket to this show." Priela hadn't meant to say the words aloud.

"My night off is Sunday. So, if that works for you, you're welcome to give my brother a hand." Jag waved the waitress down and handed her a credit card, refusing to allow Troy or Priela to pay for anything.

"I have no intention of helping. Just watching." She crossed her arms over her chest and arched a brow.

"Oh. I'm going to show you how it's done." Troy leaned over and pointed to his niece. "You see that sleeping angel? She's going to be like that all night for me."

"You're on from Sunday at noon to Monday at nine in the morning." Jag stood. "We should get going. This one will wake soon, and if we're home when she does, we can get her right into the bath where she might be happy. Take the rest of the pizza home to Darcie and Reid. If I don't see you before, I'll see you Sunday. No later than noon."

"You bet," Troy said.

"It was good to see you again, Priela." Callie took her husband's hand. "You two enjoy the rest of the night."

Priela leaned forward, resting her elbows on the table. "Have you ever babysat?"

"Not once."

"Have you ever changed a single diaper in your life?"

He shook his head.

"You might be good with her sitting on your lap for ten minutes, but you're going to be in over your head."

"I fly a jet at twice the speed of sound. I think I can handle a three-month-old little girl."

She fell back, shaking her head. "And Jag and Callie are aware of this, and they're still going to let you do it?"

"I don't think my brother ever took care of a kid until he had one of his own. If he can do it, so can I." He stuck his chin in the air as if he were insulted.

"It's different when it's your kid."

"How would you know?" he asked.

"I don't. Only I've babysat other people's kids, and it's not as easy as you think."

"Are you going to be my wingman?"

"I guess I am." She told herself that she was doing it for Stephanie's sake, not because she wanted to spend time with Troy.

And if she believed that, she had a bridge she could sell herself.

5

Troy opened the door to a private room in the library. Sitting at the table, he flipped open his computer and tapped the screen on his tablet. First, he'd watch the video a South Korean fishing vessel in the Sea of Japan had taken. Troy was by no means an expert in films, but he was one when it came to dogfights, and the Navy had tasked him to decide if what they suspected was true.

And while the aerial fight appeared to be legit, there were a few things that didn't sit well with Troy.

The first thing was how Isaac's plane had disappeared from the screen twice—and toward the west, not the north in North Korean airspace. The time-stamp on the video indicated when the foreign government believed they were being threatened. However, the enemy didn't start aggressively tailing Isaac and forcing him into the no-fly zone until three minutes later. But the enemy didn't take the first shot. Not yet. They repeated the maneuver. According to the North Koreans, they gave Isaac four warnings before shooting at him. And it wasn't a shot to kill until Isaac fired back.

A tap at the door caught Troy's attention. "Hey, Kyle, thanks for coming."

"No problem, but you could get in a shit-ton of trouble for this, Mr. Goody Two-shoes."

Unfortunately, it hadn't been that long since he'd heard the nickname. It wasn't that he didn't believe in breaking the rules, but a person shouldn't do it unless they knew and understood the rule. Had a good reason for breaking it. And most importantly, were willing to take responsibility for breaking the rule. Without those three key ingredients, they were either stupid, arrogant, or both.

Troy prided himself on being neither. However, he had been accused of being cocky on occasion. But what fighter pilot who ended up in Delta Force didn't have a slight attitude?

"I'm willing to deal with the consequences."

"You must like this girl."

"My feelings for Priela have nothing to do with why I'm doing this," he said, pushing his laptop in front of Kyle. "Studying this incident is actually part of my current assignment, which is twofold."

"You don't say. Please elaborate." Kyle clicked the play button and watched with his elbows on the table.

"My superiors have never believed that Isaac crossed into North Korean airspace. He was on a typical recon run, preparing for a mission called *Operation Pins and Needles* when he went ahead of his squadron. He was the team leader, and it was his responsibility to fly the line. But his wingman hung back, and I don't know why."

"So, that's not standard procedure?"

"No. A pilot rarely flies solo so close to enemy lines. Not on a recon mission like that. If they were going to be dropping below the radar or trying to cross into North Korean airspace, the situation might be different. But the directive that day was to run normal flybys."

"Where's the radio feed?"

"That's the other thing. Isaac lost comms for five minutes, which was enough time for the enemy to engage without Manny seeing anything, since he was out of sight." He pointed to the first shots the enemy fired over North Korea. "It doesn't matter that they fired first. Nor does Isaac appear to be the aggressor. But his wingman, Manny, just entered enemy airspace, which I find odd since there wasn't a jet on him, just Isaac."

"But there was definitely conflict in the air."

"Agreed," Troy said. "Isaac's comms came back online just as five more enemy fighter jets appeared. Isaac and Manny took out three before Isaac went down." He tapped the screen. "That's my team and me. As the rest of the enemy bugs out, so do we."

"Did we ever recover Isaac and his plane?"

"Not all of the plane, but they were able to bring Isaac's remains home."

"That's something." Kyle rubbed the back of his neck. "I don't know what I'm looking at."

"What I really need from you are your contacts."

Kyle arched a brow. "As in who? Because I think you know more people than I do at this point."

"I don't know too many people willing to skirt the system, and I can't ask without potentially raising a few red flags."

"That makes sense. So, what exactly do you want to know?"

"Manny was up to re-enlist six months later, but he didn't. He was a career Navy man and on my track. He wasn't the kind of person to leave."

"Are you saying the Navy covered something up?"

"I'm saying that someone fucked up and is covering their tracks. Or, perhaps, something more sinister."

"That's a mighty big accusation," Kyle said. "What is this *Operation Pins and Needles*?"

"The next day, at the same time, the entire squad would do the exact same run, only it would be a smokescreen while a special forces team put boots on the ground."

"In fucking North Korea?"

Troy nodded.

"Has our government lost its fucking mind?"

"Rumor has it they are close to having a nuke that will reach US soil. We need to see what's there. And we've had men in the country before. They just won't admit it."

"Have you always believed someone lied? Or is this a new theory since becoming smitten with Priela?"

Troy had to admit that was a fair question and something he'd been thinking about for the last two days. He prided himself on being unbiased, even when it came to himself. "Something has always bothered me about this case. I thought it was just the fact that I didn't believe Isaac was the one who broke the rules of engagement."

"So, you believe there was a mole on Isaac's team, and they tipped off the North Koreans?"

"Right now, that's the only thing that makes sense."

"You think it's this guy, Manny?"

"I think he's the one who tipped off the enemy because he was between the rest of the squadron and Isaac. So, what I'm thinking is that either someone on our team gave him that directive, or a Korean operative gave it to him."

"And you want me to use my contacts to talk to him and everyone else on Isaac's team."

"That is what I want."

"All right. I can handle that. But it won't happen at the snap of my fingers. What happens if this drags on after your two-week vacation is over?"

"I'm moving to Fort Eustis in Virginia, where I will meet my new team and go through some training before being assigned any missions—all while I work on this."

"Do you think maybe you were assigned this

task because your new commander believes what you're now starting to think?" Kyle asked.

"I don't think so because he prefaced it by saying they'd use it for training. I mean, Isaac did some serious fucking kick-ass flying. Even I'm impressed, and I'm an arrogant asshole in the air."

"At least you own it."

Troy nodded. "One thing I'm really beginning to believe, based on what I've seen on that video, is that Isaac knew the enemy was trying to draw him into their airspace and did the best he could to avoid it. Until he couldn't. And in the maneuver right before he crossed the line, he tried to turn the bird upside down. It looked like he might dive, but the enemy was prepared for that. As if they knew Isaac's style."

"Or someone was watching, giving the enemy information."

"I'm giving myself a headache." Troy rolled his neck. "I appreciate your help. If some money needs to exchange hands for services, I've got that covered."

"Don't worry about it. It won't be a problem." Kyle let out a long breath. "And now I want to talk to you about something a little more personal."

"Okay." Troy didn't like the sound of that. He

leaned back in his chair, lifting the front legs off the ground. For most of Troy's life, he'd looked up to Kyle. He was a bit of a legend, and Troy had been lucky to have him as a mentor. But there were moments when the man utterly terrified Troy. This was one of those times.

"My family has come to care a great deal for Priela since she moved to the area. She's a sweet woman with a lot of hurt lurking behind those bright eyes."

"I'm trying to help her get the answers that will ease that pain."

"I've known you for a long time, and I know you're an honorable man. You're the kind of person I'd want to take into combat."

"But not someone you want hanging around any female you care about," Troy said with a tinge of a bitter taste in his mouth. He swallowed, but it only got worse. Not because his buddy had insulted him, but because his old friend was right.

"That's not what I'm saying at all. I know you better than you know yourself, and you're hiding behind your dedication to your career."

"I mean no disrespect, but you can stop now." Troy had heard this argument a million times from his parents and his brother, Jag. And as of late, Darcie and even Reid had started in on him.

"No. You're going to let me finish."

"All right." Troy could at least hear what his friend had to say. It wouldn't change the fact that Troy's life wasn't conducive to a long-term relationship.

"I saw you fall hard for a girl a long time ago."

"Ginny," Troy whispered. It was no secret that he'd loved Ginny and she'd loved him, but no matter how hard they tried, they just couldn't make it work. "She's married now and has a kid. She's very happy."

"I'm aware. But you've used that breakup as the backbone of your single status."

"That's not entirely true." Troy let the chair drop to all fours. "I had just graduated from the academy and was being deployed for the first time when we broke up."

"Because she wasn't cut out for being a military wife. But that's not true of every woman."

Troy opened his mouth, but Kyle kept talking.

"I know the divorce rate is high. I've seen it with my friends. It's a stressful life. But when it works, it's amazing, and I saw the way you and Priela looked at each other. And I heard all about your day visiting Fort Casey and pizza after."

Troy jerked his head back. "Excuse me? Is the entire town gossiping about me? Or worse, Priela?" His pulse increased to dangerous levels. It took a lot to ruffle his feathers, and it only happened when someone fucked with his family. This was new territory for him, but he sure as shit didn't like the idea of people talking about Priela.

"No. She told my wife and me. And during the exchange, Priela's eyes lit up like a damn Christmas tree. I'm sure she wasn't even aware. And maybe you were tasked with this particular job, but when you're on leave, you're a creature of habit. Find a girl, have a little fun, then leave."

"I'm not doing that with Priela. I consider her a friend, and I want to help." Troy did his best to rein in his frustration. He certainly understood Kyle's concerns. Troy and Jag had felt similar ones when Reid first came back into Darcie's life. While they knew they were meant for each other, their first attempt at a relationship hadn't ended well.

But this was different.

Troy wouldn't let his attraction get in the way. There would be no more kissing. Ever. He could control his lips.

"Here's the thing. I think—and others agree—that you and Priela are a match."

"Oh, for fuck's sake. You sound like my mother."

"Your mother's a smart woman." Kyle smiled. "I honestly never in a million years thought I'd say a lady was a good fit for you because you're so high-maintenance. And let's face it, a bit of a womanizer—"

"I take offense to the last part of that statement."

"There isn't another word for a man who has a string of short-lived, monogamous one-night stands."

"I take offense to the term *one-night stand*. I might not do long term, but when I'm with a woman, even if only for a week, I'm committed for those seven days." Troy arched his brow. "But I get your meaning, and I respect Priela too much to use her like that."

"Damn. You're in bigger trouble than I thought." Kyle pushed his chair back. "I've always considered you family, and I think you and Priela would be good together." He held up his hand. "I just want you to start thinking about what's really important in life."

Troy stood and gave Kyle a bro hug. "I know you mean well, and you know I love ya for it."

"I'll be in touch." Kyle stepped out of the small room and disappeared into the library.

Running a hand through his hair, Troy blew out a long breath as he plopped back down into the insanely uncomfortable wooden chair. He could deal with attraction. What he struggled with were feelings. It's why he never allowed himself to become attached.

Only Priela had his eye for the next two weeks, and he couldn't turn away if he tried. Even if nothing happened, he'd dedicate his time in Seattle to what she needed.

6

———

Troy twisted the cap off a water bottle and chugged while he listened to his sister Ziggy discuss some of the stories the news program she produced was working on. It was nice to see his sibling so animated. He certainly didn't understand why their mother was so worried about her eldest child. Ziggy appeared to be happy and thriving.

And so was Troy.

He glanced around his parents' backyard at his family and close friends. It would be like this almost every night until he left. His mom and dad sat on the swing, being ridiculously cute. It was sweet how much they were still in love with each other. Darcie had plopped herself on her husband's lap in front of the fire pit. Again, another insanely happy couple. And, of course, there was Jag, who seemed to be the biggest hands-on dad ever, and Callie always so relaxed and at ease.

Being around his family gave Troy great comfort. He tried to come home as often as possible because it started to affect him psychologically if he went past six months. All he needed was a short dose, and it would last him another six months. But he had to have that connection.

"Your sister speaks faster than anyone I know," his buddy, Dustin, whispered.

Troy laughed. "I know."

"She's mad-wicked smart, though."

"I can guarantee she's almost always the smartest woman in the room."

"Does she have a boyfriend?"

"Not that I know of, but she's pretty private when it comes to her love life." Troy tried to remember the last time he'd met one of Ziggy's guy friends. It had been a few years.

"I know someone who's interested in her."

Troy cocked his head. "Really? Who?"

"One of my pilots. He's a nice guy and an ex-Marine. When he's not flying for me, he's a firefighter."

"Sounds like a stand-up dude. I'll ask her."

"I heard you're going to attempt babysitting with the help of a pretty lady." Dustin smiled as if he'd won the lottery. "I don't know which I find more amusing. The fact that you think you can handle a baby or that you believe Priela will fall for your charm."

"My entire goal in life is to make sure you find humor." Troy wouldn't give either topic life. He had to admit that he was a little nervous that his niece would beat him down and make him look like a fool.

When it came to Priela… He knew she was way out of his league, and he kept telling himself that he should keep his distance. The mere fact that she worked for Daisy's family should prevent him from stopping by the restaurant tonight.

But he knew he would because waiting for her in her driveway would feel even more stalkerish.

"I have a favor to ask." Troy had no intention of losing the bet. He would still take Priela to dinner, but he was going to do it on his terms.

"What's that?"

"Can I borrow a plane?"

Dustin laughed. "You act as if it's like asking if you can use my car."

"I don't need a big jet. Do you still have your little four-seater? I just need something to take Priela to Lake Tahoe."

"Are you really doing this with her?"

"Doing what?" Troy asked, and a flare of anger laced the question.

"Dating her for the ten days and then ending it."

"That's fucking harsh." Troy glanced at his watch. It was too early to go to the restaurant. He'd already done some recon to find out when the last meal would be served and when Priela would be off work. "And that's not what I'm doing."

"I didn't mean to offend you. It certainly wasn't a dig." Dustin squeezed his shoulder. "It's just who you've been since you and Ginny broke up. If you were home for a month, you'd stick with her for that long, but then you'd end it as soon as you left."

"You make it sound like I use the girls I date." If he weren't driving, he'd be snagging a beer. He hadn't realized his sex life had been the topic of so many conversations that hadn't included him. "I'm not some womanizing bastard. I'm not going to hurt Priela."

"I never said you were. But let's face it. Priela

isn't the kind of girl you normally date. She's more of a Ginny."

"They aren't anything alike." Troy wished he didn't understand what Dustin was getting at, but he did.

"But they are in the ways that affect your heart," Dustin said. "I'm not concerned about her. It's you I'm worried about."

"What the hell does that mean?" He glared at his longtime friend.

"I know you don't believe this, but Ginny broke your heart, and you've been pretending that you're better off being single ever since. When, deep down, you don't want to be, and Priela is exactly the kind of woman you'll fall in love with."

"I've been home for three days, and you, Kyle, and my family all have me in love with Priela. Hell, my mother had that happening before I even came home. Why is that?"

"Because she's perfect for you."

"Then you don't know her very well," Troy said, letting out a long breath. "She hates the military."

"That's not true, and you know it."

Troy cocked his head. "Please. She resents the hell out of what happened to her brother." And if she ever knew Troy had been there that day, she'd probably kill him with her bare hands. He should probably drive right past the restaurant and go straight to Darcie and Reid's.

"Maybe so, but all she needs is a little help to get past that."

"I can't give her the answers she needs. And trust me, I'm trying to find something, but I have to be careful."

"I know." Dustin waved at his wife. "I transport a lot of rich people who have a lot of power in certain circles. One happens to be a retired Army general who now owns a private security and special operations company. He does a lot of dirty jobs, if you know what I mean."

"Are you going to be seeing him anytime soon?"

"Tuesday. He booked me to take him back and forth to San Diego. The flight leaves at eight in the morning, and we fly back at six in the evening. Want to fly with me? I can make the introductions."

"I'd love to," Troy said. "I'd still like to borrow one of your planes either next Thursday or Monday."

"I can make that happen." Dustin slapped him on the shoulder. "But I want you to do me a favor."

"Oh, shit. Here we go." Troy rolled his eyes. "What do you want?"

"At the end of your leave, I want you to be totally honest with yourself and Priela about how you really feel."

Troy opened his mouth, and his heart dropped to his gut. His answer should have come quick and easy since he should have no problem being honest about that. Yet… He cleared his throat. "You say that as if you know she and I are going to be an item."

"If you're taking her for a picnic lunch or dinner in Lake Tahoe, then you're definitely interested," Dustin said. "I need to go spend some time with my wife. I'll talk to you later."

Shit. Dustin was right. Troy wanted Priela, and he knew he wouldn't stop thinking about her while he was home. He could tell himself that it was because of her brother, but that was only part of it. She'd gotten under his skin in a way that no woman had since Ginny.

He glanced at his watch.

Fuck it. It might be a little early to go to her work, but he could have a soda at the bar while he waited.

He strolled to where his parents were seated. "I'm going to head out."

"So soon?" His mother jumped to her feet and wrapped her arms around him. "I'll be out on the island tomorrow in the afternoon. I'd like to stop by and see my granddaughter."

"Just text me when the ferry docks." He kissed his mother's cheek and shook his dad's hand. "Thanks for dinner."

"Drive safe, son."

He said his goodbyes to everyone else as quickly as possible and then hopped on his brother's Harley. It would take him a good twenty minutes to get to the restaurant. He shouldn't have to wait too long. So, as he pulled out onto the highway, he told himself to take a nice, leisurely ride. However, every time he glanced down at the speedometer, he saw he was going at least ten to fifteen miles over the speed limit.

By the time he got off the highway and was cruising down the speedway toward the docks, he realized he would be a good fifteen minutes early. Of course, Priela had no idea he was coming at all. Unfortunately, that meant he would have to deal with Daisy.

That turned his stomach.

He parked the bike and took a deep breath. Daisy always gave him heartburn. He had once cared for her deeply, but he hadn't truly loved her. And he always felt bad for leading her on that way. He hadn't been mature enough to call it quits when he should have.

As he pulled open the door, he braced himself for the onslaught of tantalizing aromas. The restaurant was known for fresh local seafood and great steak, and Troy didn't think the menu had changed in a decade. Nor had the décor, which wasn't necessary. It had a rustic seaside grace to it, as many of the locally owned places did.

"Troy. What brings you by?" Daisy greeted him with a big smile and open arms.

Inwardly, he groaned. He was so tired of the pretenses. "I'm here to see Priela." He took a step back.

Daisy paused, dropping her hands to her sides. "You don't need to be so cold," she said quietly.

"Yeah. Actually, I do. You don't respect my boundaries and still let our parents play this game with us after all these years, when you know damn well you and I won't ever even be friends. You destroyed that."

"You certainly know how to hold a grudge."

"It's not about that." He hadn't had this conversation in a good three years, and he never thought he'd need to have it again. "You could have ruined my life with that lie."

"But I didn't, and it's time to move past it."

"I have. Now, can you please let Priela know I've stopped by to see her?"

"Wait right here." Daisy turned on her heel and stormed off toward the kitchen.

Talking to Daisy never went well, and God only knew what she'd tell Priela. Hopefully, nothing too horrible. And something easily explained.

Priela plated the last six meals and sent them out of the kitchen. She loved being a chef, but she'd much prefer working on her own menu, not one where she had to stifle her creativity to bend to the flavors the owner wanted. What was even worse was that she wasn't the head chef. She was actually at the bottom of the barrel and only worked a few nights a week because her catering business was more important to her. Though she *would* like to own her own restaurant that was attached to her business.

She'd taken this job because of the flexible

hours, so she shouldn't complain. It added credibility. And, hopefully, when the time came to take out the loans she needed, it would give her all the experience, as well as helping her put money in the bank so she'd have the capital she needed.

However, she knew she was a few years away from that goal, and that was if she stayed in the area, something she wasn't sure she'd be able to do.

For her, that was the rub. Having grown up as the kid of a squid, she'd learned to enjoy moving every couple of years and figured she'd get the itch to change scenery in about three years. Which meant, she might never actually open that restaurant.

And that might be okay. She loved her catering business, but it would be hard to relocate that every few years.

Then again, moving around the country would allow her to learn about different types of food.

She wiped her hands on her apron after she cleaned the counter. Today had been a long day, and she looked forward to going home, sitting out on her patio, and watching the ferry take its last few runs across the Sound as she sipped a glass of wine before going to bed.

"Hey, Priela?" Daisy, the manager, stepped into

the kitchen. "Someone's here to see you."

"Who?"

"Troy Bowie. Why is he coming here to see you?"

"I've done work for his family," Priela said.

"I know that. I was at the party his family threw for him the other night." Daisy put her hand on her hip. "Please don't tell me that you're hooking up with him."

Technically, Daisy wasn't her boss, but she was the owner's daughter, so Priela had to play nice in the sandbox and not tell her to go fuck herself. "I'm catering his niece's christening." She left it at that.

"I'd be careful when it comes to Troy."

"What does that mean?" Priela asked.

"Because he'll break your heart." Daisy tilted her head and fiddled with a lock of her hair. "He's never gotten over me, and this is his way of trying to get my attention. But until he makes some changes, he and I can't be together."

It took a lot of energy not to burst out laughing. "Well, I'm not interested, so you have nothing to worry about," Priela said. "You can tell him I'll be right out."

Daisy narrowed her stare. "I'll seat him at the bar."

Priela flattened her hand over her stomach, trying to calm the jittery butterflies. Quickly, she checked the time. Ten thirty. Maybe he had some information about her brother. But he could have called.

"I'll be right out," she said, smoothing down her slacks. She raced to the bathroom and freshened her makeup. There wasn't much she could do with her hair since it had been under a hairnet all day, so it would have to stay in a ponytail. She stared at herself for a long minute. "Don't overthink this. He's just being a nice guy. Besides, not only aren't you ready for a man in your life, but you don't want a military man or a player." She dabbed a little gloss on her lips and strolled out into the main room. There were only two full tables left and three people sitting at the bar, including Troy. "What are you doing here?" she asked.

He hopped off the stool and pulled her in for a hug, kissing her cheek. "I was at my folks' for dinner and was headed back to my sister's when I remembered that you said you were working tonight. So I thought I'd stop by and say hello."

"That was nice of you."

"Looks like you're about done." He winked.

She tilted her head.

"Okay, so I knew when the restaurant stopped serving, and I might have timed my little visit." He held her hand, rubbing his thumb over her skin. "I wanted to see you again."

Her heart swelled, and that scared her. She wished he didn't have such a powerful impact on her senses. "We're getting together tomorrow so I can watch you crash and burn at babysitting."

His dark eyes twinkled with mischief. "Let's make a little wager."

"What kind of bet?"

"If I can handle it, you have to cook me dinner. And I don't mean just any dinner. I want your best."

"And if you have to beg me for help, like I know you will?"

"Then I'll take you to any restaurant you want, anywhere in the United States," he said with a grin.

"How do you plan on doing that?"

"I'll borrow my friend's private jet and fly you first class."

"You're on." She gave him a little jab in the arm. "I was just about to head home and watch the ferry cross the Sound while having a glass of wine. You're welcome to join me." She held up her finger. "For one glass before you go back to Darcie's."

"I like that idea." He placed his hand on the small of her back and guided her toward the door. "I take it you walked?"

"I did."

"I'm not sure how I feel about you doing that this late at night."

"I often get a ride home from one of the staff members in the kitchen." She climbed on the back of his bike and wrapped her arms around his strong middle, resisting the urge to rest her head on his shoulder.

"That makes me feel better." He turned the key on the Harley and eased out into traffic. It took all of five minutes for Troy to pull into her driveway. "Other than being on the main drag, this looks like a great place."

"It was an awesome find. I got it fully furnished, and the rent is dirt cheap for Seattle." She was way too aware that he was only inches behind her as she climbed the steps of her porch. She used the keypad to unlock the door. The lights flickered, much like the butterflies still fluttering in her midsection. It had been a long time since a man had made her feel like a schoolgirl with a crush. "Make yourself at home."

"Wow. This place is beyond amazing." He

fingered the back of the plush leather sofa. "And you really can see the Sound." He pointed toward the water.

"But you can hear the honking horns and the announcements as well."

"I guess that would be a bummer."

"It is when I'm trying to sleep, but I love being near the water." She pulled down two wineglasses. "Is Pinot Noir okay with you?"

"That's perfect." He stood with his hands in his pockets and stared out the sliding glass door. "How many bedrooms does this place have?"

"Two, but one is really small. I use it for an office." She handed him a glass. "I rented it for the view and the kitchen." She pointed over her shoulder. "It takes up most of the space and has a double oven. Not to mention, the size of the freezer and the fridge. It makes it easy to run my catering business out of here."

He turned. "Holy shit. My mom would love it."

"She's been here a couple of times to pick up meals."

"You've cooked meals for my folks?" He arched a brow.

"For her ladies' groups, like a book club."

"Ah. Yeah. She stresses over shit like that. I'm

glad she's finally letting someone else do that kind of stuff for her. My sister told me she finally hired a cleaning lady." He opened the sliders.

The cool, salty air hit her face and reminded her of all the reasons she loved being at sea. "It took my brother dying for me to finally get one of those." She took a long sip. "I'm sorry, that sounded rude."

"Not at all. How are your parents doing?"

"It depends on the day. For the most part, they try to live their lives without letting their grief overwhelm them, but my mom struggles. The statements the Navy made beat her down."

"I can imagine."

"My dad, however, accepts it."

"He doesn't believe it, though, does he?" Troy set his wine on the small table. He did the same with her glass before running his hands up and down her forearms.

"No. But he respects their version of the story and thinks I should, too. He's even gone as far as to say that Isaac would want me to, and that just pisses me off." She blinked. "Would you want your family toeing the military line if it was you who'd died?"

"I'm not sure I can answer that question honestly anymore."

"Why?"

"You and your brother have changed my perspective." He cupped her cheeks. "I spent today going over the Navy's statement and called in a few favors."

"What does that mean?"

"I think something stinks." He tenderly brushed his lips over hers.

But she pulled away. "You don't get to say that and then not elaborate."

"I can't. Not until I know more."

"That's so unfair." She folded her arms across her chest. "Why wouldn't you share what you know?"

"Because right now, all I have are theories, guesses, and more unanswered questions. You have to trust that I'm taking this seriously."

"I do, but I don't like being in the dark."

"When I know something substantial, I'll tell you." He took her chin with his thumb and forefinger. "I promise."

Letting her body relax, she rested her hands on his hips. Everything about this man made her want to curl up on his lap and let him take care of everything. And that freaked her out. She'd never been very good at relationships, and they never lasted very long. She'd dated one man while in culinary school for about a year, but as soon as she decided to move, he did whatever he could to talk her out of it and wouldn't hear trying to make things work long-distance.

Truth be told, she had been relieved when they broke up, and even more so that he hadn't once tried to contact her since she'd come to Seattle.

Without allowing herself to think about what she was doing or what it might or might not mean, she slipped her fingers under Troy's shirt. She splayed her hands across his back, leaning into his hard chest.

His warm tongue eased between her lips like a soft feather. Kissing him was like tasting the finest of foods and drinking only the best wine. "I'm sorry." She scurried across the patio and snagged her wine.

"What's wrong?"

"Don't take this the wrong way, but your reputation for being a player precedes you. And to be frank, while I'm all for short-lived affairs—it's kind of the only way I roll—I do a lot of work for your family. They're actually my biggest repeat customers."

"I see." He leaned against the railing, gulping

from his glass. "I never thought of myself in those terms, but I guess others do."

She laughed. "The female version of that would be called a slut."

"That's cruel."

"I know." She laughed. "It's not that you're only going to be here for a short time and this would only be sex. I can handle that. Honestly, I'd prefer that because relationships are too complicated and messy. It's the way one of the waitresses at the restaurant called you out on it. I don't want to be seen as a notch in Troy Bowie's belt."

"I wouldn't want you to be known for anything other than being you." He downed the rest of his wine. "I need another one of these after hearing that."

"Help yourself." Priela plopped herself down on the lounge chair and put her feet up. She hadn't wanted to break off that kiss. If she were completely honest, she would have loved to strip him naked and make love to him right on the chair.

Her entire body heated for about a second until she remembered that waitress telling her how everyone knew that Troy was pursuing her, and that lip-lock proved it. So, was helping her just a way to get into her pants?

No. He wasn't like that. He couldn't be.

He reappeared, carrying the bottle. "Do you want more?"

She held out her glass.

"Not that I care all that much about what people say, but can I ask exactly what was said and by whom?"

"Daisy. The manager of the restaurant."

"Shit, well, that explains a lot." After filling his glass, he dragged one of the chairs from the table closer.

"Why? Was she one of the *girls* you played?"

"No. I dated her in high school for two years."

"Seriously?"

He nodded. "She thought when I left for the academy, we'd be able to make it work, but I had no desire, and she became a problem for a while."

"How so?" Priela kicked off her shoes, tucked her feet under her butt, and pulled a fleece blanket over her legs.

"She was always trying to win me back, and I made the mistake of hooking up with her a few times."

"You're a bad boy." She waggled her finger.

"I can be." He laughed. "In my defense, I was young, stupid, and horny. And she was my first."

"We always remember our firsts." She nodded.

"I'd sometimes like to forget. She lied to me about something huge, and I've never told my parents what she did. Which is why they keep putting her in front of me."

"What did she do?"

"It's a two-part story," he said. "First, she tried to trap me with a fake pregnancy."

"That's a shitty thing to do."

"I'd appreciate it if you kept that to yourself. Her parents are friends with mine, and I'd rather not go down that road. Besides, when I was about to quit the Naval Academy because of the baby, Daisy actually came clean, and I promised her I wouldn't tell and asked her not to either."

"That's very respectful of you," she said.

"I was also embarrassed that I fell for it," he admitted. "And then, while I was away at college, I met and fell in love for the first and only time. It made Daisy batshit crazy. When I brought Ginny home to meet my family, Daisy did anything she could to break us up, including telling Ginny that I made Daisy have an abortion—which I never did."

"Did Ginny believe her? Is that why you broke up?"

"No. Ginny and I were solid."

"Then what happened to you and Ginny?" Priela found herself leaning closer and gazing into his eyes once again. She would end up in his arms if she weren't careful. Although, she was beginning to think that wouldn't be too terrible.

"She wasn't cut out to be a military wife. My first deployment ended our relationship. She's happily married with a kid now."

"Good for her."

"What about you?"

She shrugged. "Not much to tell. I never had time for boys growing up, and with moving around all the time, I just didn't get attached to people very often."

"Have you ever been in love?"

"I don't think so," she admitted. "I've always been focused on my career."

"And now your brother."

"That's true." She dropped her head back and sipped her wine. "Did Ginny break your heart?"

"I wouldn't say that. I was hurt, but it was for the best, and we both knew it. Since then, I guess I've been what Daisy described to you. But she makes me sound like some kind of predator or something. I'm not like that. I never date more than one woman—"

Priela held up her hand. "You don't have to explain yourself to me. I don't think I'm any different."

"I guess we're two peas in a pod." He leaned over and tapped his glass with hers and then winked.

She laughed. "Did we just talk ourselves into you spending the night here?"

"If we didn't, we'd have a different problem. I'm sure I'm over the legal limit, so I'd have to wait it out at least an hour, and that would mean I'd miss the last ferry." His lips were less than an inch from hers. "And for the record. I didn't do that on purpose."

"I wouldn't hold it against you if you did." She palmed his cheek. Her heart hammered in her chest, and her skin burned as if someone had lit her on fire. "Shall we go upstairs?"

"Why, Priela Sloane, are you propositioning me?"

"I'm hoping to take advantage of you." She stood, letting the blanket fall to the patio. She handed him her wineglass and pulled her shirt over her head. "Follow me." When it came to sex, she'd never been shy, but it wasn't something she took lightly either. She didn't jump into bed with just anyone. She might not want to have big, messy, emotional relationships, but she didn't want to have different bed partners on a regular basis, either.

If she could have a regular friend with benefits, she'd do it. Hell, she'd tried it a few times, but feelings always got in the way. Not on her part, but once a man wanted more from her, she had to end it.

Troy managed to unhook her bra as she climbed the stairs, so she let it drop to her feet as she turned to face him at the edge of her bed.

Since the place had come furnished, she hadn't spent too much time making the place hers. Instead, she'd put as much money as she could into her savings so she could continue growing her business.

About the only thing she'd bought was her bamboo sheets and comforter. It felt weird to use someone else's.

Troy traced a path around her belly button and to the swell of her breast with his index finger. He stared at her as if he'd never seen a half-naked woman before.

She reached for his belt buckle and loosened it, tugging it from his jeans.

He ripped off his shirt and yanked her to his bare chest. His mouth crash-landed on hers in a desperate, messy encounter that had only one purpose: to ignite the rest of her body.

And it did that and more.

She gripped his shoulders, digging her nails into his muscles, scraping them down his back before slipping her fingers into his pants to cup his ass.

He dotted sweet kisses on her neck before taking her breast and rolling his tongue over the tight, sensitive nipple.

She allowed herself to get lost in his touch. Typically, she'd want to control all aspects of any sexual encounter. It didn't have to do with power, but she hadn't felt as though she was in the driver's seat for most of her life. Sex gave her that sensation.

But with Troy, she didn't want it. She actually enjoyed giving it all to him, and he certainly didn't disappoint.

Rolling her slacks over her hips and down her legs, he gently laid her on the bed. "You're exquisite." He stood at the edge, removing the rest of his clothing.

"You're not so bad yourself."

"I'm glad you like what you see." He climbed in next to her, his fingers dancing across her skin, his tongue doing wildly wicked things to all the right places.

Every time she tried to take a deep breath, she couldn't feel her lungs. Deep moans filled the back of her throat. She'd lost all control of her senses, and she relished the wildness of his lovemaking.

It was tender but eager, and she selfishly took all that he gave.

Her climax built at the curl of her toes. She gripped his head, glancing down. It had to be the most erotic thing she'd ever experienced, and her orgasm tore through her system like a tornado touching down and rolling across the land. She couldn't have slowed it down if she tried. Her body jerked and twisted. She gasped, desperately trying to catch her breath.

"That was fun," he whispered. He kissed his way up to her neck, then rolled to his side.

"Where are you going?"

"To get protection."

"I have one in the nightstand." She opened the drawer and pulled out a condom, holding it up with a triumphant smile.

"Aren't you a regular Girl Scout?"

He tried to snag it.

She shook her head. "I get to put it on you."

He arched a brow. "I don't know why that scares me."

Sitting up, she tore open the foil package and tried not to stare too hard at him as he lay flat on his back. She took him in her hands.

He hissed.

She smiled as she covered him with the necessary barrier.

"I can't say that doing this has ever been sexy before," he said with a heavy breath.

"Might as well turn something that can kill the mood into something fun." She straddled him, taking him inside her on a slow stroke.

"Good Lord, you're going to be the death of me." He gripped her thighs and blinked.

She arched her back and rolled her hips slowly, still feeling the aftershocks from her orgasm.

His fingers crawled up her legs, hips, and landed on her nipples, tugging and twisting. He played her body like he was a master pastry chef, and she was his dough. The tension built deep in her soul.

He flipped her to her back and rose on his hands. He stared into her eyes, holding her gaze captive. His motions were intense and increased in power and force with every stroke.

She hooked her ankles around his waist and dug her fingernails into his shoulder muscles. She couldn't hold off her second orgasm any longer.

His eyelids fluttered, and he groaned as he thrust into her, long and hard, holding steady for a moment as he exploded, whispering her name. The way it rolled off his tongue made her shiver in delight.

He settled on the bed, pulling the covers over their bodies. He rolled to the side and grabbed something off the floor. "I'd better text Darcie and Reid. If I don't come home, they might call Jag and send out a search party."

Priela's cheeks heated. She pulled the covers over her face. "That might be worse than the walk of shame."

He laughed. "I never said I was going to tell them where I was staying." He set his cell on the table next to the bed. "That's none of their business."

"And you don't think they won't make an educated guess?" She snuggled against his chest.

"I'm sure they will, but I won't tell if you don't."

"Deal, but only if you promise we can do that again in the morning." She pressed her lips over his nipple.

"I was planning on it."

Priela folded one arm across her middle and sipped her coffee as she watched Troy stuff his face with the crepes she'd made him for breakfast. Besides waking in the middle of the night with an uncontrollable desire to ravish the body sleeping next to her, she hadn't been this rested in months.

Of course, that didn't account for feeling like she'd been riding a horse for two days.

The last time she'd had sex multiple times in one night had to have been… she couldn't remember when.

"I'm going to get fat hanging out with you." Troy licked his fingers as he stood and strolled across the kitchen.

"Yeah, well, I can't walk this morning."

He laughed. "Not entirely my fault." He took the mug from her hand, setting it on the counter next to her plate of fruit as he pulled her to his chest. "I'm not the one who demanded sex at three in the morning."

"I didn't demand it. And you could have just lain there and let me take care of you."

"I'll remember that next time."

"You're awfully confident I'll want a repeat performance."

"Ouch." He kissed her nose. "That hurt my feelings."

"More like bruised your ego." She gave his cheek a little pat.

"You're killing me." He reached around her and grabbed a fresh mug of coffee. "What time are you going to be able to be at Jag's?"

"I won't get there until six."

"Make sure you pack an overnight bag."

"I never said I was spending the night." She took a piece of cantaloupe from the tray and plopped it into her mouth. "I don't think your brother and his wife would appreciate that, and I'm not about to sneak out in the—"

"They are expecting you to stay over."

"Excuse me?" She poked the side of his arm.

"I mean, sleeping in the guest room, while I crash on the sofa." He winked. "They don't think I can do this alone, so they would feel better if you were there, as backup. And since you sort of agreed."

"Oh, good grief. Seriously?"

"They've asked me three times if you were coming over for sure. In order to calm their nerves, I confirmed it."

"You're such a sucker." She glanced at her watch. She had a shit-ton of cooking to do before this lunch. Not to mention, his mother would be dropping by with some party favor things for the christening next weekend. She'd almost forgotten until Henrietta had sent her a text about a half hour ago, asking if it would still be okay.

"Why do you say that?"

"They're using this babysitting thing to try to set us up. Your entire family is in on it. I first thought it was only your mother—who will be here in a half hour, by the way, so you should scoot—but they've all started drinking the Kool-Aid."

"Did you just say *scoot*?" He rinsed out his mug and put it in the dishwasher before clearing the table.

Impressive.

More so that he continued and did the rest of the pots and pans without being asked.

"I just told you that your mom is on her way, and you're stuck on word choice?"

He handed her a frying pan and a towel. "It's a funny word, and I'm not surprised about my family."

"Are they always trying to fix you up?"

"My mom is always looking, but it takes someone pretty special for the entire Bowie crew to get involved. They all adore you." He wiped his hands on his jeans.

"You take it all in stride. I think I'd go bonkers on my parents if they did that."

He shrugged. "They mean well, and since I'm always honest with the ladies I date, I'm not concerned about anyone getting too hurt."

"The operative words there being *too hurt*." She raised her hand when he opened his mouth to say something. "I get it. I'm the same way. I don't want to get too involved with any man. My problem stems from the way I grew up. I'm worried that I'm going to want to move after a few years. I mean, two years in San Diego and I was going bonkers. I loved it for about a year, and then I started to get restless."

"A Navy brat goes one of two ways. They either wander, or they find one place and stay there forever."

"My dad says you eventually get tired of it, but I can't imagine. And I like the idea of traveling and learning about different local cuisine. I've mastered some fish dishes that I hadn't even heard of before moving to Seattle. Someday, I want to go to New Orleans and check out their authentic food."

"I love New Orleans. And the food there is great." He bent over and slipped on his boots, pulling his leather jacket from the coatrack.

"I get the feeling you love all types of food."

"I love the food you keep putting in front of me." He took her in his arms and kissed her hard.

She gripped his shoulders, caving to his soft lips and tantalizing tongue. She had half a mind to strip and let him have his way with her right there on the kitchen table.

Ding-dong.

She jumped.

"Shit," she whispered, turning her head. She swallowed. "I really should put a shade on my window." She took a step back and smoothed her hair. "Your mom's here."

"I see that."

His mother waved and smiled.

"This is going to be interesting," he whispered. "Are you ready?"

"Hell, no. But go ahead." Her face flushed. If her cheeks weren't bright red, it would be a miracle. There was only one conclusion to draw from this situation, especially since she had her hair in a ponytail and wore a nightshirt and shorts.

Troy pulled open the door. "Good morning, Mom." He leaned in and kissed his mother's cheek. "I think you're early."

"I didn't know I'd be interrupting anything," his mother said. "And I wasn't expecting to see you here."

"I was just leaving. I have to stop at Darcie's before I head over to Jag's for my first date with my niece."

His mother laughed. "Yeah. You don't want to show up in the clothes you wore last night."

Priela sucked in a breath.

"Mom," Troy said. "I can't believe you just said that. Besides, I missed the ferry, so Priela was just kind enough to let me crash on her couch."

"That was very nice of you, dear. Thank you," his mother said.

Priela opened her mouth, but no words escaped her lips. She had no idea what to say. She had never been in a situation like this before in her life, and while she felt a twinge of embarrassment, she wasn't ashamed, nor did she feel overly uncomfortable—which she thought she should, considering.

"Since you're here, why don't you go down to my car and carry up the two boxes in the back seat?" his mother said.

"No problem." Troy bolted out the door.

"I'm glad he was here because those party favors are heavier than I thought." Henrietta set her purse on the table by the door. "I'm sorry if my teasing offended you or upset you in any way. We Bowies can be an odd group."

"It's fine." Priela waved her hand, thankful it didn't shake.

"I appreciate you taking care of these party favors. I know it's not in the chef's description."

"I told you I would make them partially edible, and Crystal and I are going to work on it together."

"That's amazing. I don't know what I'd do without you." Henrietta held her by the forearms, giving her a good squeeze. "My son is a good man. Don't listen to the gossip mill nonsense about him."

Priela tilted her head. "I always make up my own mind about people."

"Where do you want these?" Troy stepped into the kitchen.

"Put them both in my office at the top of the stairs." Priela pointed.

"You got it." Troy smiled before lifting the box onto his shoulder.

"I worry about him," Henrietta said.

"I don't think you need to. He's got a good head on his shoulders."

"So do you." Henrietta took her by the hands. "I bet you and Troy have a lot in common."

"Both boxes are unloaded." Troy came up behind his mom and wrapped his arms around her. "Do you need anything else?"

"Nope. But I do need to run a few more errands before I head over to the island. I'll see you later." She turned and hugged her son before disappearing out the door.

"Well, that was slightly embarrassing," Priela said.

He looped his arm around her waist and kissed her temple. "I hate to do this to you, but I have to go now if I'm going to have enough time to take a shower and pack a bag."

She patted his taut stomach. "Go. I'll see you around dinnertime. And don't worry, I'll bring food. No way could you handle cooking *and* taking care of Stephanie."

"Are you cooking, or are you getting takeout from somewhere?"

"I'm cooking."

"Wonderful." He gave her a quick kiss and pulled open the door. "Fuck," he mumbled. "We can't catch a break."

"What?" She peered over his shoulder and saw Daisy standing at the bottom of her driveway. "What the hell is she doing here?"

"I don't know. But I'm about to find out." He jogged down the steps.

Oh, this wouldn't go well. Priela snagged her fleece and slipped her feet into her boots. She charged after Troy, who practically raced across the driveway.

"Daisy, what the fuck are you doing here? I thought we finally settled all this last night." Troy planted his hands on his hips.

Shit. This was going to get ugly, and that was the last thing Priela needed at work.

"Well, I'm not here to see you, that's for sure." Daisy flipped her hair over her shoulder.

"And what business do you have with Priela?"

"She's my employee, for one," Daisy said.

"Hey," Priela interjected. "Did you need something?" she asked, trying to deflect and defuse. Anything to ease the anger radiating off Troy's body. Not much got under his skin, at least that she'd seen, but this woman certainly knew how to push his buttons.

"We have some business to discuss. I tried calling, but you didn't answer." Daisy glanced between Priela and Troy. "Now I know why."

Priela wasn't going to take the bait. She grabbed Troy's biceps and squeezed hard, making sure he didn't either.

"You could have left a message," Priela said.

"I did, but it's important." Daisy turned her attention to Troy. "Do you mind giving us a minute?"

"Whatever you need to discuss, you can do it with Troy present." For some reason, Priela felt like she needed a witness.

"Suit yourself," Daisy said. "I wanted to talk to you about your schedule and adding some shifts. Specifically, I need you to work tonight."

"I can't do that." Priela clenched her fists. When she'd taken the job, she'd been assured that she would be the swing chef, taking only a few shifts. Right now, she worked at most three nights a week and the occasional fill-in. The more catering jobs she took, the closer she came to being able to quit. However, she hadn't told them that.

"Why not? I checked around town and you don't have a catering gig."

"Actually, I do," Priela said.

"Yes. But it doesn't require you to be there. You just have to drop off the food. You could be at the restaurant at three." Daisy tilted her chin. "You agreed to cover on nights you didn't have catering jobs. We're down a chef tonight."

"I'm sorry. I can't," Priela said. "You'll have to ask one of the other chefs who is off tonight."

"That's the other thing." Daisy tucked her hair behind her ears. "We're making some changes and moving—"

"You had to come to her home and do all this here?" Troy asked. "Or did you see my brother's bike, hear about her babysitting Stephanie, and decide to come and cause problems?"

"You really think I'd do that?" Daisy gasped, covering her heart.

"You faked a pregnancy," Troy said. "I think you're capable of being a backstabbing—"

"I think what Troy is trying to say is that there are more appropriate times and places to have this conversation. Regardless, I won't be working tonight because I agreed to help Jag and Callie."

"Then you might want to rethink your employment. Because if you can't commit to five nights a week so we can have more continuity, we're going to have to let you go."

"You can't—"

Priela interrupted Troy. "Then consider this my notice." She'd had enough of Daisy, and if this was what she would have to deal with because Daisy was jealous that she was sleeping with Troy, then fuck it. Priela was too old for these kinds of games. And if she needed to, she was a good enough chef that she'd find another job.

"Don't let her force you out of a job because she's being a bitch," Troy said.

"I'm not. My catering work is picking up, and I have some other skills I can hone. I don't need her employment to make it."

"Well, in that case, Daisy, I think you can leave." Troy puffed out his chest.

Daisy drew her lips into a tight line. "I warned you about him." She turned and took two steps, then slid behind the steering wheel of her Jeep. "I'll mail you your last paycheck." She revved the engine and pulled out into traffic.

"I'm sorry about that." Troy rubbed Priela's back. "I feel bad about your job."

"Don't. I'd rather not work for someone like that anyway."

"Are you sure you're going to be okay without the income?"

She nodded. "There are other restaurants, and I'm good at what I do."

"That you are." He brushed his lips over her mouth. "I need to go."

"Drive safe." She watched as he mounted the Harley and drove off into the line of vehicles waiting to board the ferry. He turned and waved.

Her pulse increased. Her mother used to tell her that when the right man came along, it always happened when you least expected it and would change everything.

Troy couldn't be that man. There was no way Priela could fall in love with a man like Troy. He was a good person. Honorable and trustworthy. But he couldn't give her everything she wanted and desired in a partner.

That was a fact.

So why did her heart break just a little knowing that he would leave in less than two weeks?

Troy pushed open Jag's front door. "Your nanny has arrived." He took off his boots and hung up his leather coat in the front hallway.

"Hey, Troy," Callie greeted him with a hug and a kiss. "Where's your partner in crime?"

"She's got a bunch of catering things she had to take care of."

Callie frowned. "She's not coming at all?"

"She'll be here around dinnertime." He cocked his head. "You really don't think I can do this on my own."

"You've never taken care of a kid before." Callie looped her arm through his and dragged him into the family room. "I trust that you will take good care of her, but it's not easy, and while she's mostly a good baby, she can be difficult at times."

"If Darcie can handle her, then so can I."

Callie laughed. "Darcie did not have a good first experience."

"That's not what she said." Troy eased to the floor where Stephanie was in a little bouncy seat.

He tickled her fat little belly, and she gave him a big smile and a giggle.

"Do you think she's going to let you believe that she struggled, considering she's about to have a baby of her own?"

"What happened?"

"Nothing horrible. She just had no idea that it would be so exhausting. Both she and Reid are a little terrified that they aren't ready."

"It was a bit of a shock. I mean, they'd only been back together for a couple of weeks when she got pregnant. But they are the perfect couple, and they will make great parents. I'm sure of it."

"Speaking of perfect power couples," Callie said as she picked up a bunch of toys that were sprawled all over the floor.

"Let's not go down that road." Troy rubbed his temple. Getting caught with his pants down, so to speak, in front of his mother had been hard enough. He knew that information wouldn't stay quiet. Of course, his mom might have already spread the news, but he just didn't want to discuss it. He'd already had to explain to Darcie where he'd spent the night and took a decent razzing from Reid. He didn't need another one from Jag and Callie.

"And what road is that?"

Troy arched a brow. "I don't think I have to spell it out for you."

"Why are you so touchy?" Callie joined him on the floor. "You usually take this kind of harassment with such grace and style."

He wished this was the usual type of crap his family dished out when he dated a girl. But this went beyond that. And when his mother showed up this morning, he knew that everything was different.

And not just with his loved ones.

He was behaving in ways he wasn't used to, especially this morning. In the past, if he'd heard that his mother was on her way over, he wouldn't have stayed for breakfast. He wouldn't have taken the chance of getting caught red-handed, knowing that his mother had a horrible habit of being early.

Not to mention, Dustin's words hung heavily in his mind.

Priela was the kind of woman who could steal his heart, and it had taken him a long time to get over Ginny.

Too long.

If he were honest with himself, the idea of opening his heart scared the fuck out of him because he couldn't go through the kind of pain she'd caused. Not again.

Or the kind of betrayal that Daisy had created. It didn't matter that he hadn't loved Daisy; he had loved the idea of their child.

One that never existed.

Fuck. He hadn't allowed his mind to go down this path in years.

"Troy?" Callie touched his forearm. "What's going on?"

"I'm in over my head," he whispered. He hadn't meant to admit it, but he realized that he needed to talk to someone, and it couldn't be one of his siblings.

"With Priela?"

He nodded. "If you haven't heard yet, I spent the night there."

"I can't say that piece of gossip got to this house yet."

Troy leaned back on his elbows and stared at the ceiling. "My mother showed up at Priela's house, and we were in a lip-lock at the front door. Mom saw the whole thing."

"That's unfortunate because your mom isn't going to let that go easily. She loves Priela and has been talking about how perfect she is for you for months."

"Why does everyone think she's the right woman to make me change my wild ways?"

"You're not wild. You're wounded." Callie held up a rattle and waved it in front of Stephanie.

"Why would you say that?" Troy had heard everyone in his clan say that at some point, and it drove him nuts. However, he never asked them exactly what they meant by it, in part because he didn't want to know, but also because he knew they were right. He just didn't want to dig deep enough to figure out how to fix it, because that meant his life would change.

And he didn't want that.

He liked the way things were and enjoyed where his career was headed. A full-time girlfriend would alter his life in ways he wasn't prepared for. How the hell could his life be turned upside down and inside out by one woman, in the span of a long weekend? It made no sense.

Of course, when he met Ginny, he'd told his buddy that he'd met the woman he would marry. And he'd meant it.

"You keep everyone outside of us at arm's length."

He caught Callie's gaze. "I'm glad you don't feel like I shut any of you out."

"You don't. But we all watch you come home and find the one girl who isn't good for you—" She held up her hand. "Let me finish."

He nodded.

"You always believe your mom brings Daisy around because she likes her. Well, she doesn't. She invites Daisy to remind you of your bad choices."

"Do you have any idea how screwed up that sounds?"

"I do, but she's trying to play air traffic controller with your love life. She's done it with all of us, but she approaches you very differently."

Stephanie tossed her toy, and Callie found a new one and handed it to her daughter.

"The problem is, you end up picking up what Jag calls *a good-time girl*. Someone who will get over you quickly and isn't interested in any kind of long-distance relationship. Meanwhile, your mother is putting a couple of women in front of you, one of whom is a nice girl who suits you on an intellectual level. Like Priela. Only this time, she's your other half. Your soulmate. She's who you're supposed to be with. It's so obvious to everyone."

"It's not obvious to me. Or to her, for that matter."

"It never is to the two people involved." Callie pushed on the chair, giving it a little bounce as Stephanie started to fuss. "Look at me and Jag, and your sister and Reid. We all had to break up for a period of time to figure out how perfect we were for each other."

"I do like Priela, but it's not like I date women I don't care for."

"But you look at her differently than the party girls you usually bring around."

"That's how you view the women I go out with?" he asked, pushing himself to a seated position.

"I wouldn't let any of the other girls stay here with my precious little girl." She lifted Stephanie out of the seat and handed her to Troy.

He stood and placed the child over his shoulder, patting her back as he bounced up and down. She nuzzled her face into his neck.

"I don't have time for relationships, and my career makes for shitty marriages."

"That's an excuse for not taking a risk with your heart again."

"Maybe, but Priela's made it pretty clear that

I'm a nice distraction for the next few weeks. But when I'm gone, that's it. Not to mention, she lost her brother—"

"I know." Callie waved him back to the kitchen where she handed him a bottle.

He took it and sat at the table to feed the very tired little girl.

"She and I have talked about what happened to her brother. She thought maybe with my investigative skills, I might be able to help her. But I couldn't find anything, so I sent her to Kyle and mentioned she might ask you."

He closed his eyes, and the footage of the dogfight appeared. The more he recalled it, the more he believed that whoever had filmed it, purposely didn't follow Isaac's plane when it left the screen the two times it headed to the west. What happened during that time? Troy believed it was important. Along with why the video was shot in the first place and then later released.

"She's wounded, too," Callie said. "I don't know much about her past romances, so I don't know if a man hurt her in some way and that's why she's not willing to commit, or if all of it has to do with her brother."

"I get the impression it has to do with the military in general. And that's why we're so not compatible."

"Are you listening to yourself?"

"I am," he said with a slight laugh. "Like I said, I'm drowning here, and I can't see the shore." He kissed Stephanie's forehead. Looking at his niece suckle at a bottle made his heart melt. There was nothing sweeter than holding this little angel. Watching his older brother with his family and seeing his little sister pregnant had changed something in Troy. He wasn't exactly sure what was happening, but he now questioned his life choices.

And being with Priela only intensified those inquiries.

"Have you talked to Priela?"

"Sort of. I mean, she was pretty candid with me about her brother, and since she had words with Daisy at work, I had to tell her about that whole situation."

"Shit. I forgot she works there."

"Not anymore. She quit." He set the bottle on the table and lifted the sleeping baby onto his shoulder to gently pat her back, hoping to show off and get a burp out of her without waking her up. "Regardless, I'm being reassigned to a team in Virginia. My career choice isn't going to change."

"And it shouldn't. Being in a relationship doesn't mean you should give up your life. But it does mean you make compromises so you can both have what you want." Callie leaned against the counter. "Look at me and Jag. I'm still writing full-time, and Jag is still the chief of police. The only difference is that Jag isn't going to take a different position that would move us, and neither am I. And Darcie and Reid are starting a brand-new business together, but she'll continue taking out some charters, and he'll still run extreme sports. You can still be in Delta Force and have a relationship."

"Maybe, but I doubt it would be okay with Priela." The sound of footsteps coming down the stairs caught his attention.

"Finally, your brother is ready. I swear he takes longer to shower and pack than I do."

"I thought I heard you down here," Jag said softly. He kissed his daughter's forehead and patted her back. "You can put her down in her crib. She'll sleep until about three. But after that, other than a short nap around dinner, she's up until about ten, and she's not always happy."

Callie put a small binder on the table. "This has everything you need to know, and don't hesitate to call us with any questions. Your mom is stopping by, and Darcie can be here at the drop—"

"Relax. I've got this." Troy smiled. "Now, go and enjoy a romantic night together. Maybe you'll make another one of these."

"Bite your tongue," Callie said. "We are so not ready for that."

"Agreed." Jag looped his arm around his wife. "We'll see you around nine in the morning."

Troy waited for them to drive away before heading up the stairs. "Okay, little one. Please stay asleep." Gently, he bent over and set her in the crib, wrapping her in the blanket.

She barely moved, except to let out a big exhale.

He stood over the crib and stared down at the sleeping baby. When Jag had called to tell him that Stephanie had been born, Jag had said that he didn't know he could love another human being so much.

Troy didn't pretend to understand that concept. Stephanie wasn't his child, but the love that filled his heart for the baby was like nothing he'd ever experienced.

He made sure the baby monitor was on and quietly slipped from Stephanie's room, then headed to the kitchen where he set up his laptop and pulled out all the information he had on Isaac so far, along with some new intel that had come in, though it hadn't told him anything he hadn't already known.

What he wanted to do was talk with Priela's father.

He found Benjamin Sloane's email address.

Dear Commander Sloane,

My name is Captain Troy Bowie, Delta Force, E Squadron (aviation) and I'm friends with your daughter, Priela. I'm reaching out to you because I will be in San Diego for a few hours on Tuesday. I have a very short window to meet, but I'd like to talk to you about your son. I need to keep this between us—

Fuck. Troy deleted the email. He couldn't send that. There would be a record, and that could get him fired.

For treason.

He set his cell on the table and tapped the phone number for the commander. It rang three times.

"Hello?" a man answered.

"Is this Commander Sloane?"

"Yes. Who is this?"

"My name is Captain Troy Bowie with the E Squadron of Delta Force."

"Do I know you?" Commander Sloane asked.

"No, sir, you do not. But I am friends with your daughter."

"Priela? Is she okay?"

"Yes, sir. She's fine. I'm not calling about her." Troy rubbed his temple. He hadn't thought this out too well, which wasn't like him. Still, it was better than ambushing the man at his house. "I want to unofficially—and off the record—talk to you about Isaac."

"Did my daughter put you up to this?"

"Yes and no."

"I don't like cryptic, son. So don't talk in circles."

Troy could respect that. "Sir, I could be court-martialed for this. I need to be a little secretive."

"All right. But how do I know you're who you say you are?"

"My brother, Jagar Bowie, is the chief of police in the city of Langley. You can call him. Or you can call Detective Albert Morning of the Seattle Police Department. But I can't give you my commander because if he knew I called you, I'd be toast."

"Why?"

"I think you know why."

"All right. What do you want?"

"What I'm about to tell you, I'm going to beg you not to tell Priela. At least, not yet," Troy said.

"I don't like keeping secrets from my family," the commander said.

"I understand, but I started my career as a fighter pilot with the Navy, and I've been tasked to study the footage from Isaac's accident." Troy played the video on his computer screen. "I was asked to do this before I knew Priela, whom I met through my family."

"Hang on a second," the commander said. "Hey, honey. Are the Bowies the family that Priela does all that catering for that she talks about? I think the mom's name is Henrietta, and one of the kids is married to that guy who owns the extreme sports company."

Troy smiled. It was nice to know his family had made an impact, and hopefully a good one.

"Yeah. My daughter speaks highly of your family."

"The feeling is mutual," Troy said.

"Why haven't you told Priela about what you're doing?"

"National security, among other things."

"Why are you telling me?" the commander asked.

Troy liked the commander's bluntness, but it did unnerve him a bit. "I told Priela I'd see if I could look into her brother's incident, but she doesn't know that I was already doing it. I was asked to do so for training purposes, but as I looked at it more closely and tried to find an answer that Priela could live with, I—"

"Priela needs to understand that the Navy often does things we don't understand."

"I agree, but I've watched the video a million times now, and it's raised a few questions that don't sit right with me."

"No offense, son. I'm sure you're very good at what you do, and Delta Force is nothing to sneeze at, but don't you think many other trained professionals have looked at it and have drawn the appropriate conclusions?"

Not if someone was covering something up. "I'd rather discuss most of this in person, if that's possible."

"I can tell where this is going, and that's an awfully big accusation, son. Not to mention a very dangerous one."

"I'm aware. And to be honest, it wasn't easy to make this phone call. I'm literally putting my career on the line." An email came over from Kyle. Troy tapped the icon. All it said was, *Read this*, with an attachment.

"I'll meet you."

"Thank you. I'll send you the details later today."

"See you then, Captain." The line went dead.

Troy let out a long breath. He hadn't realized that his hands were shaking. He felt like a shit going behind Priela's back, and he wondered if he should tell her what he was doing. But he honestly wanted her father's opinion before he brought his thoughts to her.

He clicked on the file that Kyle had sent.

It was an obituary for Manny. He'd killed himself three months after leaving the Navy, only nine months after the incident. There had been an inquiry, as the death had been suspicious, but it was ultimately ruled as suicide.

That was a big red flag.

"Manny, what did you do?"

Troy tapped his cell, pulling up Kyle's contact information.

"Hey, man. You got my email?" Kyle asked.

"I did."

"I was about to send you another one," Kyle said. "I'm hitting send now."

"What is it?" Troy asked.

"Two names. One is Samuel Weston, and the other is Waylon King. Do they ring a bell?"

"Never heard of them. Who are they?"

"They were both part of the planning of *Operation Pins and Needles* and Weston was close to Manny."

"Are they both still active duty?"

"Since *Pins and Needles* was sidelined, they were pulled Stateside and are stationed in Pensacola. Rumor has it they are working on a new, similar mission with a new team."

"Why wouldn't they do that in South Korea?"

"My contact says they will be heading out in a few weeks."

Troy rubbed the back of his neck. "What do you know about these two men?"

"Not much. I'm working on getting their military records, but that's not always easy, especially doing it from the outside. I do know that Weston went to the Naval Academy, long before your time. He was a bit of a hothead and always had a bit of trouble with authority. But it appears he's had a solid career. Not much on King."

"Okay, thanks," Troy said. "Keep me posted."

"I'll keep digging."

Troy leaned back in the chair. Something about that mission didn't sit right, but he didn't have all the information, and until he had all the pieces, it was like finding a needle in a haystack.

8

———

Troy held Stephanie as best he could with one hand while he took the kitchen faucet sprayer with the other. He made sure the water wasn't too hot or too cold before pressing the button. "How could so much poop come from your little body?" He tried not to breathe as he doused her bottom, which was still covered in runny crap. When he lifted her from the pack-and-play and found her all wet, he'd figured she'd wet through her diaper.

He hadn't expected that she'd shit through it also.

She smiled and giggled as the water sprayed him, too.

"I'm glad you find this so funny, but now I have a ton of laundry to do as well."

The doorbell rang.

"Door's open," he yelled, trying to keep all the water in the sink, not on the counter, the baby, or on him. So far, he'd done a pretty good job.

"Oh, good grief. What is going on in here?" Priela set a few bags on the table. She raced to his side and held up a towel.

"Someone soiled herself like I've never seen before."

"So, why are you cleaning her up in the sink?"

"Because all her clothes and toys are in the bathtub."

"I'm not even going to ask why." She wrapped Stephanie in a towel and cradled her in her arms.

"You're early."

"Looks like it's a good thing." She kissed the baby's forehead. "I take it she just woke up from a nap?"

"No."

Priela arched a brow.

"She was playing in that thing in the family room with her favorite toys. Since it's getting close to bottle and naptime, I figured I'd better change her diaper, only I found all this, everywhere. And when I say everywhere, I mean diapers really don't keep this stuff in."

"Okay. Why don't I get her dressed, and you can take care of the dirty shit and put on some dry clothes?" She waggled her finger in his direction.

"Are you saying I look a little out of sorts?"

"No. I'm saying you have poop on your shirt."

He glanced down. "Gross. I can't believe what comes out of her."

"I know. The first time I watched my cousin's kid, I was mortified."

"I'll be back down shortly. The bottles are in the fridge, and I brought down diapers and extra clothes for her. They're in the family room."

Troy leaned in and kissed his niece and then stole a passionate one from Priela. "Mmm, that was nice."

"I would agree. Only, you smell."

"I'll be back in a jiffy." He raced up the stairs. The second he stepped into the bathroom, he gagged. He quickly grabbed all the bedding and stuffed it into the washing machine. He stripped, cleaned himself up, and tossed his clothes in with the baby's, borrowing a pair of his brother's sweats and a T-shirt. Thank God, they were about the same size.

By the time he made his way back to the family room, Priela sat in the rocking chair, reading to Stephanie. The baby stared up at Priela with big eyes. She held Priela's hand as they rocked back and forth.

He leaned against the doorjamb, unable to tear his gaze from the mesmerizing picture that graced his vision. His pulse increased. New emotions that he had no label for swirled around in his belly. It was rare that he ever got butterflies in his gut, but it seemed to be an everyday occurrence when it came to Priela.

She tilted her head. "How long have you been standing there?"

"A couple of minutes," he said. "You're amazing with her."

"I'm just reading a book. It's not that hard."

"I know, but you look at her so lovingly, and she's of no relation to you." At his coming-home party, he'd seen a lot of people holding Stephanie, and they all cooed at her—who didn't adore a cute little baby? But not everyone had that twinkle in their eye as Priela did.

"I love kids." She set the book on the table and handed Stephanie a different toy to play with.

"Do you want to have some of your own?"

"Maybe. Someday. But I'd have to find the right guy, and that's not easy with the way I want to live my life."

Stephanie tossed the little teddy to the floor, laughing.

"Hey there, sweet girl." He pushed from the wall and spread a blanket out on the floor. He lifted Stephanie from Priela and placed her on her back. He put the little toy that had dangly things from it over her, and she immediately giggled and reached for them. "What constitutes the *right guy*?"

"I don't know. I haven't given it that much thought. Between trying to get my career off the ground and dealing with my brother's death, I haven't spent that much time dating since I got out of the Navy."

"I can relate to that."

He sprawled out on the floor, resting his head on a hand.

Priela did the same, keeping Stephanie between them. "You don't have a problem dating."

He laughed. "I have a problem picking the right women."

She arched a brow. "Outside of Daisy, I doubt that."

Stephanie kicked her little feet and made a

couple of fussing noises. He took one of the toys and waved it in front of her face. She grabbed it, stuffed it into her mouth, and chewed.

"I'm starting to think maybe my family is right, and I'm avoiding real commitment."

"I thought that was by design."

"I suppose you're right, but maybe I don't want to constantly go from one short-lived relationship to another. I mean, don't you ever want to find out what it's like to be in love?"

"Of course, I do. But, and this comes from one of the few people I've dated for any length of time, I'm kind of closed off, hard to get to know, and I like to do things my way."

"I would only agree with the last part of that statement."

"That's sweet of you to say, but I have to wonder if there's something wrong with me. I mean, to be going on twenty-nine and to have never been in love… that's weird."

"Not really. And maybe you have been, but you've just never allowed yourself to feel it."

She sat up and fiddled with one of Stephanie's toys. "No. I didn't date much in high school. I mean, I had mad-wicked crushes on a couple of boys, but my dad moved us three times between the time I was thirteen and eighteen."

"That's tough."

"I found it to be adventurous. The first move was from Pensacola to Italy. Then we went to Germany for a year. I actually graduated from high school in South Korea."

His heart lurched to the back of his throat. "You lived in South Korea?"

"My dad was stationed there until my sophomore year of college," she said. "Interestingly enough, my brother was stationed there for two years."

"When was that?"

"About a year before he died. He'd been transferred back to the States for training."

"Was that with the same squadron?"

"I believe so. Why?"

Troy pushed himself back to a seated position and handed Stephanie the toy she'd just thrown. "I'm not sure, but I'm finding some things that don't add up."

"With my brother's death?"

He nodded, glancing at the ceiling. "I don't want to say too much because I have more questions than I have answers, and I could be completely wrong."

"Look at me." Priela tapped his knee. "Whatever you tell me, I will keep to myself."

"I don't want to give you misleading information. I think that would be worse than what you have now." And he needed to find out what her father knew. Because the fact that they had been stationed in South Korea changed things.

A great deal.

"But you think the Navy lied to me."

"No. I actually don't believe that. But I don't believe the military was given all the information, either. And until I get some reports back and talk to a few more people, I don't want to say much more."

Stephanie's face turned beet red, and she let out a big cry.

Troy lifted her into his arms and bounced her, while Priela handed her toy after toy, but she'd only bite them and then toss them to the floor.

"I really hate it when you do this." Priela stood and paced. "I know you're doing me a favor and putting your job on the line for me, but you could at least stop talking in circles. Isaac wouldn't cross enemy lines unless his life depended on it, and the last time I spoke with him, he was acting all paranoid."

"Okay, wait a second. You didn't tell me that."

She pinched the bridge of her nose. "Because if I did, you'd probably think he created the conflict that cost him his life."

He turned the crying baby around, holding her like Callie had shown him, putting a little pressure on her belly, which seemed to help calm her down for a bit.

"What was he paranoid about?"

"I don't know, exactly. But he was concerned about his upcoming mission. He could never talk extensively about it, and he wouldn't put anything in writing."

Shit. This would have been good to know when he started the investigation. Now might be a good time to fill Priela in on some of his thoughts. "Did he ever mention a guy by the name of Manny?"

She stopped pacing and glared. "What do you know about him?"

"I know he died by suicide nine months after your brother passed."

Covering her mouth, she gasped. "I didn't know that."

"Was he friends with Isaac?"

"They butted heads a lot, but they were on the same team, and Isaac tried to get along with everyone."

"But he didn't, did he?"

"Not near the end. The more paranoid he became, the more he and Manny butted heads. He told me that he was trying, but he said he didn't trust Manny."

Stephanie started to fuss again.

Priela stepped into the kitchen and found a cold teething ring, then handed it to the little girl.

"Anything else?"

"He didn't give me details."

"When was the last time you spoke with Isaac?"

"Three months before he died," Priela said.

"That was a month before he was deployed." A million more questions ran through Troy's mind. "Did you know this Manny fella?"

"No. I never met him, but my brother said he was a cocky son of a bitch. And he didn't like to play second fiddle."

"I know a few men like that."

Stephanie continued to fuss.

Troy decided it was close enough to bottle and naptime, so he took the bottle from the fridge and heated it up.

"What are you thinking?" Priela sat on the sofa next to him, holding Stephanie's hand as he fed her, and she dozed off in his arms.

"Because of the nature of the mission your brother was on, there are a lot of details I can't tell you, and that's not me talking in circles. I just can't. But after watching the footage of your brother's dogfight a million times and discussing it with a few people, I think the Navy might have missed some things in their investigation."

"Missed what?"

"Can you trust that I want to get to the bottom of this for you? That I'm invested in this and am on your side."

She nodded.

"I really can't say more. Not until I have additional information that I can use to back up my suspicions."

She swiped the tears that rolled down her cheeks. "I can't thank you enough for this. I'm sorry I'm being so difficult and emotional."

He set the bottle on the table and patted Stephanie's back. "You have nothing to be sorry about."

She took the baby and set her in the bouncy seat. Jag didn't want Stephanie taking her short nap in her crib. He'd mentioned that if she did that, she'd sleep too long, and the night would be hellish.

Troy didn't want to experience that.

Once he was sure the baby wouldn't wake right away, he took Priela into his arms. He ran his hands up and down her back and kissed her temple. "I'm doing the best I can to get to the bottom of this."

"I know you are." She dropped her head to his shoulder. "You're the first person who has ever taken me seriously when it comes to Isaac. Even my father doesn't understand."

Somehow, Troy doubted that. Especially after their phone conversation. But he'd reserve judgment until after a face-to-face meeting. He still believed her father was holding something back. He understood why, but it broke his heart because of what it was doing to Priela. "Maybe he understands more than you think, and he just can't tell you."

She tilted her head. "I wish that were true, but he's always toed the military line."

He cupped her face. "I know you don't want to hear this, but sometimes there really isn't anything wrong with that."

"I do know that. I just don't believe my brother's death happened the way the Navy—"

He pressed his finger to her plump lips. "I can

say with some certainty that the Navy isn't covering anything up. The problem is, they don't have the right information, and I'm starting to think that Manny might not have been one of the good guys." He knew he was speaking out of turn, but he couldn't stand to see her in such pain even a second longer. "I don't know this for sure, but I'm going to get to the bottom of it."

"You don't have to say any more." She kissed his neck. "I won't ask you to tell me anything else. You'll fill me in when you can. If you can." She caught his gaze. "I don't want you to get into trouble. I really don't."

"I have no intention of that happening." He took her mouth in a hot, passionate kiss. He hoisted her ass up onto the counter and wrapped her legs around his waist. He grappled with her bra clasp. All he wanted was to feel her bare skin against his, and he figured they probably had only ten to fifteen minutes before they were interrupted again.

He was being insanely selfish, but she didn't seem to care as she yanked his shirt over his head and tossed it to the floor. Hers followed a second later. He tried not to be so desperate, but he couldn't help himself. He needed to be inside her. To love her. To show her that someone understood and cared for her in ways that no one else did.

He wanted to be the kind of man she could count on. For the first time since Ginny, the desire to take care of someone else was stronger than his need to put himself first. And while that scared the crap out of him, he embraced it like he never had before.

Priela had opened his eyes and soul to emotions he'd been stifling for years, and being with her made him vulnerable. He ran the risk of having his heart torn right out of his chest.

But he didn't care.

Not anymore.

He finally realized that he hadn't been living but simply running on pure octane. And that wasn't enough.

No sooner did he work the top button on her slacks loose than his niece decided to wake up with an ear-piercing scream.

"Shit," he mumbled. "I guess her nap is over." He found Priela's bra and shirt and handed them to her before turning his attention to his niece. "I guess we'll have to take that up later."

She laughed. "According to your brother's

notes, she's going to be up and fussy until she cries herself to sleep around eleven."

"Oh, that's going to suck," he mumbled, staring at the clock that blinked seven in the evening.

Priela rolled to her side, resting her arm around Stephanie and Troy. Sleeping with the baby in their bed probably wasn't the best move, but it was the only way they could get the little girl to calm down.

"Good morning," Troy whispered.

"What time is it?" she asked.

"Just after eight."

"Wow. I can't believe we all slept that long."

"We didn't fall asleep until two in the morning." He kept his hand on Stephanie's belly, rubbing gently. "And she was restless for a few hours past that."

"True." She kissed the little girl's head, taking in a good whiff of her fresh baby smell, which was a combination of spring and strawberries. "But over-all, we weren't total failures."

"I did sort of crash and burn."

"Not really. She's teething and I think she's got some colic issues."

"Well, I wouldn't have been able to do it without you, so I owe you dinner."

She smiled. "It's not necessary."

"Oh. But it is. And I've got the perfect place."

The sound of the front door opening and closing startled Priela. "Did you hear that?"

"I did," Troy said, slipping from the bed. He hiked up a pair of shorts over his underwear. "I didn't expect them home this early."

"This is almost as embarrassing as having your mom catching us sucking face at my front door."

"Well, in their notes, they did suggest that if she was fussy, to let her fall asleep with me."

"Yeah. But they didn't say to let her sleep with the two of us in a bed together all night."

Someone tapped at the door.

She protectively wrapped her arm around Stephanie, who stirred. "This isn't good."

Troy raced around the bed. He slowly opened the door, but only a crack. "We're still sleeping," he said quietly. "And your daughter had a rough night with teething, which caused diarrhea. She's in here with us. Sorry, but that's the only way she was getting any sleep."

Jag laughed. "Why don't you hand Stephanie

out here to me, and you and Priela can get another hour or so of sleep if you want."

"Sounds good to me." Troy leaned across Priela and carefully lifted Stephanie off the bed.

"I need to leave by nine thirty," Priela whispered.

"Not a problem." Troy carried Stephanie across the room and handed her off to Jag before climbing back into bed. He curled around Priela, snuggling up behind her, holding her tight.

"We are not fooling around with your brother and his wife in the next room."

"Okay." He kissed her shoulder. "What are your plans for today?"

"I have to cater a dinner downtown, and I need to do a bunch of shopping for it."

"Is it going to be a late night for you?"

"At least ten or eleven," she said.

"Is there anything I can do for you?"

"You're doing it by helping me with my brother's death." She wrapped her arms around his strong body.

"On Tuesday, I'm taking a flight with my buddy Dustin and meeting with a retired general who runs a special operations company. He might know some details about Manny, so after this cuddle this morning, I might not see you until I get back."

She shivered. "Will you be gone overnight?"

"No. I leave early in the morning and should be back by eight or so."

"Can you come to my place when you get back?" She peered into his caring eyes. She hated how much she needed him right at this moment.

"I'll make sure to come right over, and I'll call you on the way home if I know anything."

"You can wait until I see you in person." She cupped his face. "I'd rather hear then."

"If that's what you want."

"It is." She allowed herself to get lost in his embrace. "I'm starting to feel things for you that I've never felt before."

"Is that good or bad?" he asked.

"I honestly don't know." She stared into his kind eyes. "This is new territory for me, and I'm worried about what will happen when you go back to Hawaii."

"I'm only there for a couple of weeks before I relocate to Virginia."

"And then what?"

"I have training for a good month before a possible deployment."

"And where will you go when deployed?"

"I have no idea." He kissed her nose. "I care about you, Priela. In a way that I haven't cared for someone in a long time."

"I've never cared for a man the way I do you. And to be totally honest, I don't know what to do with these feelings."

He pulled her closer. "You don't have to do anything with them right now."

"I feel guilty about that."

"You shouldn't," he said. "We just met, and neither of us was looking for this or knows what to do with a relationship. Let's enjoy what we have during the time I'm here and deal with any kind of future, if we want it, when that time comes."

"I love that you're so practical, but it also freaks me right the fuck out."

"Why?" he asked.

"Because I'm thinking that I might want to see what that future looks like."

"Yeah. That scares me, too." He rolled to his side, keeping his arm around her body. "I haven't maintained a relationship while in service, and I don't know how to do that."

"I have no idea either, but lots of people do it, so it can't be that hard."

"I think *hard* is a relative term," she said as she slipped from the bed. "I should get ready to go."

He propped himself up on the pillows. "I don't think I'll see you now until tomorrow night, and that really sucks."

She leaned over and gave him a quick kiss. "I hate to admit that I agree."

He groaned. "I need a cold shower."

"I'm sure your brother can accommodate. I'm going to head home. I'll see you at my place tomorrow." She gathered up her belongings and stuffed them into her bag. "Thanks for being one of the good guys."

"Trust me, had my niece not been wedged between us, you'd be calling me a very bad boy."

She laughed. "That, I know to be a fact." She left Troy in bed and tiptoed down the hallway, hoping she didn't draw attention to herself. She gathered all her belongings in the kitchen. All she needed was a cup of coffee to go, and she'd be on her way to catch the next ferry.

"Where are you sneaking off to?" Callie asked.

"Shit, you scared me." Priela jumped as she placed her to-go mug under the coffee machine. "And for the record, I'm not being sneaky. I'm trying not to wake the sweet child who turned into a demon last night."

"Ah. You met my real kid."

"I still think she's adorable. She's just teething and has colic."

"You don't say," Callie said as she rubbed the back of her neck. "Thank you so much for staying the night. I know she can be a handful, and I doubt Troy would have lasted the entire night without the help."

"Oh. He would have," Priela said. "Your house might have been destroyed, but he and Stephanie would have been fine without me. The only thing I did was feed him."

"Are you saying my brother-in-law could have handled Stephanie on his own?"

Priela nodded. "It wouldn't have been pretty, but they both would have survived."

"Wow. I'm impressed."

"You and me both." Priela twisted the cap on her mug. "I need to get going. Maybe we can catch up tomorrow for lunch?"

"Oh. I'd like that. My mother-in-law has been asking when she can take the baby for a few hours, so that would be awesome. We could have a glass of wine and do lunch at Rosie's if you're up for it."

"I'm down for that. How about I meet you there at twelve thirty?"

"Works for me," Callie said. "I can't thank you enough for babysitting."

"I hope you and Jag had a good date night."

Callie smiled widely. "It was amazing. We haven't had a night like that since before we got married."

"You deserve a few stress-free nights."

"Yeah, except with our luck, we made another baby."

Priela gasped. "Seriously? I thought you weren't ready for that."

"We're not. But when you choose not to use birth control, shit happens." Callie waved her hand. "I'm so tired of condoms, I told Jag to fucking forget them, and he was all too ready to oblige. And without having a baby in our bed half the night, we fucked like rabbits."

"That was more information than I ever needed to know."

Callie opened the fridge and pulled out some orange juice. "Only I know my cycle, and I bet I'm fertile as heck right now."

"That doesn't mean you got pregnant."

"But it doesn't mean I didn't." Callie leaned

against the counter and swigged from the carton. Well, it was *her* house.

"We do want to have another child; we just thought we'd wait another year."

"You sound like you're not planning on waiting anymore."

"Nope." Callie set the carton on the counter. "Even if I'm not pregnant this time, we decided there's no point in waiting. We're not getting any younger. We want our kids to be close, and maybe we want more than two." She shrugged. "I just worry about this teething thing."

"They do outgrow it."

"That really isn't making me feel better." Callie sighed. "I just worry we're making so many rookie mistakes, like letting Stephanie sleep with us sometimes, that we're not going to be able to handle two."

"Oh. You don't need to stress over that. You'll break Stephanie of that as well as any new baby that comes your way. My cousin went through similar things, and it all worked out. It's stressful and hard, but you'll work it out."

"I hope so." Callie hugged Priela. "Thanks for the pep talk."

"Anytime," Priela said. "I'll see you tomorrow, then."

Before anything else could happen or be brought up, Priela stepped out of the quaint house and climbed into her small SUV. She gripped the steering wheel and sucked in a deep breath.

In five days, she'd managed to find out what true love felt like, and she didn't want to let it go.

But she would have to if she wanted to survive. Loving Troy would only lead to heartbreak—and not necessarily hers. No way could she be responsible for causing that kind of pain and grief. Not after she'd heard what he'd already been through with Daisy and Ginny. She couldn't do that to Troy. And if she stuck around, that's exactly what would happen because even if she really was in love with him, she couldn't stay committed.

She was incapable. She knew that to be a fact. Her track record proved it.

9

Troy glanced at his cell. No messages from Kyle or Dustin. He stuffed his phone back into his fleece's pocket and zipped it, protecting it from the elements.

He leaned back and tilted his face toward the sun. It was ten degrees cooler out in the middle of the Sound as Darcie and Reid's sailboat cut through the water at about a six-degree heel, which was a decent ride.

Darcie stood behind the steering wheel while Reid was down below, getting a couple of drinks.

"Here you go." Reid appeared from the galley and handed Troy a beer and Darcie a flavored water. "You look like you're anywhere but relaxing on this boat."

"I've been working on a special assignment for the Navy that ended up overlapping with a favor for a friend, and it's giving me a fucking headache."

"I was worried something bad had happened with Priela." Darcie took a long sip of her water. "Like you offended her and she told you to take a hike."

"What is it about Priela that has you agreeing with Mom?" Troy honestly wanted to know what his family really saw in her that made them believe she was the one for him. He needed to understand why confusion swirled in his heart and why he desperately wanted to let Priela into his soul. He'd never met a woman who'd taken up this much space in his mind. Up until this morning, he'd told himself that it was her brother's story that'd pushed her under his skin. But being around her while babysitting his niece had fundamentally changed the way he viewed his life.

Only he wasn't exactly sure what he wanted his future to entail. He knew he didn't necessarily want his career path to change, but he found himself willing to make adjustments if that meant Priela would continue being in his life. And that was frightening.

"She's the female version of you," Darcie said. "Minus your love of all things Navy."

"Yeah. That's a problem," he admitted. "But that's misdirected."

"It seems pretty black and white with the way her brother died." Reid adjusted the main sheet as the wind died down a bit.

"But it's not, and I might be onto something that could uncover something pretty bad. It would prove the mission was compromised, and her brother a pawn, forcing the United States to cancel a top-secret mission."

"Wow. You really shouldn't have told us that," Darcie said.

Troy rubbed his temple. "I know. But I've never felt this helpless before. I can't use my security clearance to check on this. Not yet. It would raise such a big red flag on what I'm trying to find out, and I don't know who all the players are yet, or who the bad guy is. Except for maybe one, and he's dead."

"I don't understand why you can't dig, officially."

"Because I was tasked to study the tactical maneuvers for training purposes. Her brother was a badass in the air. He did some amazing flying before he went down. The Navy wants to use that.

They already released their final report on his death. While they don't blame him, at least officially for the incident, they do recognize that he flew into enemy airspace."

"So, the military is essentially saying he fucked up, it was a mistake, and he paid for it with his life," Reid said.

"Exactly."

"And you no longer believe that?" Darcie said.

"No. But I don't have enough information to prove that someone might have been working with the enemy to shut down the mission that was set to happen the very next day."

"So, this incident was a diversion?" Reid tugged the sheet one more time before securing it on the fleet.

Troy nodded. His cell buzzed. Quickly, he pulled it from his pocket. He smiled.

Priela*: Have fun sailing. I'm making you a chicken salad sandwich and will get some treats from Crystal's bakery for your flight tomorrow. Jag will drop it off at Darcie's tonight.*

Troy: *Thanks. But you didn't have to do that.*

Priela: *Don't take this the wrong way. It was left over from a job I did today. :)*

Troy: *I still appreciate it. See you tomorrow night.*

"What has you so happy?" his sister asked.

"Excuse me?" He glanced up, relaxing his face that hurt from grinning. He wiped a hand over his scruff. His cheeks flushed. The last time a woman had had this kind of effect on him had been in college. He wasn't used to it, but he had to admit, it was kind of fun to have his heart flutter a little faster and his belly turn to mush at the thought of Priela.

Only, he didn't like how it turned to stone when he allowed his mind to wander to the days after he left to go back to the base. Or worse, when he was deployed.

Or worst case, if she didn't want to try a relationship with a career Navy man.

Fuck. Did he really just have that thought?

He inhaled the salty wind, letting it sting his lungs. "I'm fucked," he mumbled.

Reid slapped him on the back. "No. You've just met your match, and you're both in odd places in life. Darcie and I know all about that."

"It's not like I'm in love with this woman. I just met her." Troy turned to the side and stared at the horizon. A few of the sun's rays cut through the low-hanging broken clouds and beat down on the dark water. A gust of wind caught the sail, pushing the boat a little faster.

"Love has so many levels." Reid leaned back on the bench, resting one arm over the back. "Personally, I believe in love at first sight because the second I laid eyes on your sister, I was head over heels, and I knew it. I just didn't know how to deal with it. Besides the age difference—"

"You're not that much older," Darcie interjected.

"I don't know, ten years is a big gap, and he is an old man." Troy laughed. "Older than any of us."

"Be careful, kid. I might toss you overboard." Reid took a long draw from his beer. "As I was saying, I loved your sister the moment I met her. But love grows, and that first initial attraction that makes you feel out of your element and unsure can often be confusing. And, sometimes, we brush it off as infatuation or sexual tension."

"What are you? A shrink now?" Troy rolled his neck. He resented that everything Reid said made perfect fucking sense, especially the part about being uncertain. The hard part was that this shouldn't feel like uncharted waters for Troy. It wasn't as if he hadn't had real feelings for a woman before. He'd cared deeply for Daisy before she turned into a crazy person, and he'd truly loved

Ginny. So, what the hell was he so afraid of when it came to Priela?

He blinked.

He knew the answer. Allowing the thought that she might never return those feelings crushed his heart in such a way that he knew he might never recover. The more he let her in, the harder it would be.

The worst part was that he suspected it was too late to even try to close the gate.

Reid chuckled. "No. But I know Ginny fucked with your head. And I can relate to that. When Erin died, I closed myself off to the idea of ever being with anyone again. I know you don't believe you've done that because of what happened—"

Troy waved his hand as if it were a white flag. "No. You're right. I've totally shut myself off and only picked *party girl* types to date. I know that. I just thought I was doing it because I didn't want to hurt another woman like I was hurt. I didn't know I was doing it to protect my own heart."

"That's no way to live, big brother," Darcie said.

"The thing is, I've been perfectly happy with my life. Truly happy. I love my job, and this move to Virginia with Delta Force is a good thing. I didn't expect this to happen with Priela."

"True love is always unexpected," Reid said.

"I'm not in love with her." Only, the more Troy tried to tell himself and them that, the more he realized that he was falling head over heels. How the fuck was that even possible? "I just really like her."

"That's a start," Reid said. "Now, is there any way I can help you with this investigation? My company supplies a lot of equipment to ex-military organizations."

"Really? Do you know an ex-special forces man by the name of Decker Griggs?"

"The co-owner of the Aegis Network with Brian Asher?"

"That's the one," Troy said.

"I know him well. I've been supplying him with safety equipment and other gear for five years now. He's an odd man. But he's one of the good guys."

"I'm meeting with him tomorrow to discuss the possibility of him helping me get to the bottom of what might have happened to Isaac."

"He does more extraction and protection-type jobs, but I'm sure he'd be happy to help. Would you like me to give him a call?"

"Dustin is introducing me to him on a private

flight tomorrow," Troy said. "Maybe you can come with?"

"Do you really want to read me in on what you're looking for, considering how much you're now putting your career on the line?"

"If I'm wrong, and I get found out… worst case, they'll court-martial me. Best case, they'll discharge me without honors. But if I'm right… Who knows what the Navy will do? They could make me a hero, or they could bury my career, depending on who gave the enemy the information about the top-secret mission."

"Shit," Reid said. "You're saying someone on Isaac's team was a traitor?"

"I think it goes deeper than that." Troy chugged the rest of his beer. If he were going to find out what really happened to Priela's brother, he needed help, and it wasn't going to be through Navy channels. He might as well call on those he really trusted. "I'm pretty sure the person who gave the intel to the North Koreans about the routine flight pattern is dead. He died by suicide nine months after the incident, but the coroner originally ruled his death as suspicious."

"What makes you think he tipped them off?" Reid asked.

"Because Manny was Isaac's wingman, but he wasn't anywhere near him when the fight went down, nor did he have working comms during the beginning of the dogfight. He showed only after shots were fired. Because they tasked me to only focus on Isaac, I didn't look at Manny's flying maneuvers. Once I did that, I saw a disturbing pattern."

"And what was that?" Reid asked.

"Manny should have been shot down at least twice, but the enemy pretty much stayed away. And all the North Korean planes that were hit, were from Isaac. And then the rest of his squadron and my team chased them away."

"Wait, what?" Darcie screeched. "You were there? Does Priela know?"

Troy shook his head. "And I don't want her to know until I have all the facts, okay?"

"Oh, boy. That's not going to go over well," Reid said, taking his empty beer bottle and placing it in the recycle box. He snagged a second beer. "That's not the kind of shit you want to keep from the lady you're falling in love with. Trust me when I say that will backfire on you in the worst way. You need to tell her as soon as possible."

"Not yet. Not until I know what happened and

who was responsible." He caught Reid's gaze. "I don't think this was a rogue man selling plans to the enemy. I think this goes higher than that, and I'm worried that even her father knows."

"Why do you say that?" Reid asked.

"They were stationed in South Korea for years. The mission they stopped was to put men on the ground in North Korea."

"Jesus. That's dangerous," Reid said. "Have we ever even done that?"

"That, I can't answer."

"Fair enough." Reid nodded.

"None of this can be repeated." Troy caught his sister's gaze.

"I haven't heard a thing," she said. "But you're crazy to keep any of this from Priela. I'd have my husband's head on a platter if I asked him to look into something for me, and he chose to keep me in the dark."

"But I don't have any answers," Troy said.

Darcie cocked her head. "You're lying to her about things, and that's one way to kill the possibility of a future."

"She's right," Reid said. "You should at least tell her that you were there, and you should do it before we get on that plane tomorrow morning."

Priela snagged a spoon, took her bowl of ice cream, and plopped herself down on the sofa. She pointed the clicker and turned on the television. Some good reality TV was exactly what she needed. She pulled the blanket up over her flannel pants and dove into her decadent chocolate treat, just as the doorbell rang.

"Who the hell could that be?" She glanced at her watch. It was only nine, but still. No one she knew would just drop by. She scurried to the front door and smiled when she saw Troy standing on the other side. "What are you doing here?"

He stepped inside and kissed her as if he held the weight of the world on his shoulders. "I wanted to talk to you about a few things before I leave tomorrow."

"You sound so serious. I don't like that."

When he took her by the hand, she noted that he had his laptop tucked under his other arm. He led her to the kitchen table and pulled back a chair. "I'm going to show you some things I really shouldn't, and I need you to promise me you will never breathe a word to anyone. Not your parents. Not your diary. Not your best friend. The only person you can talk to about this is me."

"Now you're scaring me." She looked up. "What is all this about?"

He had drawn his lips into a tight line, and she saw tension in his face she'd never seen before. His eyes were dark and filled with tortured pain.

"I don't mean to frighten you. I've been carrying this secret around with me ever since I met you, and it's killing me inside. I can't do it anymore." He sat down and slid his chair close. He flipped open his laptop. "I need you to swear to me this stays between us or I have to walk out that door. I'd lose my career over this."

She hadn't known Troy long, but this was not the way he rolled. "I promise."

"What you are about to see is the actual footage

of your brother's dogfight. Not what was released to the press."

She gasped, clutching her chest. "Does it prove my brother didn't do what they are saying?"

"No. It still shows he crossed over into enemy airspace."

That wasn't the answer she wanted to hear.

Troy tapped on the keyboard. "I want you to know that when we first met, the only reason I didn't tell you about this was because I couldn't. I'm still breaking so many rules, it could get me court-martialed."

She pressed her finger over his lips. "I don't want to ruin your career. If you don't want to show me this, then don't, especially if it sides with the Navy and their statements." She swallowed a sob. She'd be strong. Troy wouldn't lie to her, only a few minutes ago he'd mentioned a secret he'd kept since he'd met her.

He'd known about this all along.

She narrowed her stare. "You knew my brother broke the rules of engagement all along and you let me go and on with my anger and you didn't tell me?"

"It's not like that." He took her chin with his thumb and forefinger. "The Navy tasked me with studying your brother's dogfight when I left my SEAL team and was recruited by Delta Force and the Special Tactics Squadron. I will be spending more time analyzing fighter pilots and maneuvers and facilitating training than I will be going out there on missions."

"Get to the point, Troy."

"Your brother was one of the best damn pilots the Navy has ever seen. What he did up there that day is nothing short of amazing, and his superiors know it. They couldn't give him a medal or clear his name because of what this video shows, but the Navy's focus has been narrow-minded. They only had me looking at Isaac's tactical maneuvers for future training purposes so something like this doesn't happen again. They never gave me the AAR, the after-action report, so I don't know why Manny was so far behind or why he left Isaac's side."

She pinched the bridge of her nose. She'd been a cook in the Navy. While she understood the jargon, she didn't get half of what was coming out of Troy's mouth or why it was relevant. "You're confusing me. Please slow down and stop talking in circles." She fought the tears that threatened to break free. "Can't you request the AAR?"

"I did, which will open an interesting can of worms since the reason why I asked for it is out of the scope of my current assignment."

She took in a deep breath through her nose and let it out slowly. She categorized the new facts, but it sounded like a bunch of the same old bullshit. However, it was the intensity in his words that had her heart hammering in her throat. "Is that going to get you in trouble?"

"No," he said. "I've explained what I saw and why I felt it was important to national security. You have to understand that I hold two roles. I'm in an intelligence position with Delta Force as well as a tactical flying instructor."

"That sounds like you get split in different directions a lot."

"Not really. I work with teams to strategize the best way to get our men in and out of dangerous situations in the air, but we're digressing." He tapped the screen. "Okay. This is your brother's plane. He has no wingman, and that was the first red flag for me and it has bugged me from the beginning. According to the reports I was given, he lost comms with the ship for five minutes. But he also lost comms with Manny and the rest of the squadron. But why wasn't Manny at his side? My wingman would never leave me. Not unless he was shot out of the sky."

"Doesn't the report tell you that?"

"Yes and no. Manny's statement says that Isaac ordered him to hang back. But no one else on that squadron has ever said that. I don't have full confirmation, but I have talked with one of the men that did say he never heard the order." His finger moved across the screen. "You see here where Manny comes into the dogfight. But he's not engaging. That doesn't make sense."

She leaned forward. She hadn't been a pilot when she was in the Navy, and when she'd done her tour on a battleship, she'd done it in the kitchen as a cook. Therefore, she wasn't exactly sure what she was looking at.

"Manny's maneuvers are weak, and what is more disturbing is that the enemy constantly misses when they fire."

"But they don't miss my brother's plane, do they?" She swiped at her face.

"And they hit two other jets as well." He tapped the screen as more fighter jets appeared, and then the enemy turned around and bugged out.

"That's more than just Isaac's squadron," she whispered. "We were never told that another team was in the area. That's more sailors who saw what happened."

"They only saw the tail end," Troy said. "See that plane there." He pointed.

"Yes."

"That's me," he said. "My team and I were in the area. When the fight broke out, we were called in as backup, but by the time we got there, it was over, and Isaac's plane was—well, going down."

She flattened her hands on the table and stared at the screen. Her heart beat so fast, she wasn't sure if it would explode or only jump right out of her chest. She couldn't fill her lungs, and it wasn't for lack of trying.

"You were there?" she questioned with an unsteady voice. "You watched Isaac's plane crash into the Sea of Japan, and you didn't think I'd want to know that?"

"I couldn't tell you." He pressed his hand on her shoulder.

She shrugged it off.

"Priela. You have to understand that this incident is a matter of national security and I could end up in military prison for the rest of my life for telling you this."

"I get that's something you wouldn't mention

the first time we met." Rage filled her veins like a wildfire ripping through a dry forest. "I understand that you can't discuss some things about your job and that there would be no reason under normal circumstances for you to tell me any of this. I'm also not an idiot and you haven't told me anything about the mission. Why you or my brother's team was even there. I don't know the details, so there is literally nothing for me to repeat. All I want is for my brother to have the respect that he deserves. And you shit on his memory by keeping at least the knowledge that you were there." She dared to catch his gaze. As gracefully as she could, she pushed the chair back and stood. She needed a little space or she might actually haul off and hit the man. "Even after you agreed to help me, I might have accepted some secrecy. But the second we slept together… Actually, before you accepted *my* invitation into *my* bed, you should have told me you were there and that just maybe you knew my brother was the scapegoat."

"I'm telling you now."

"You're telling me out of guilt and that doesn't make it okay." Tempted to pick up the chair and throw it at him, she took a step back. "Jesus, Troy. You were there the day my brother died. Do you have any idea how it makes me feel to know that you've been lying to me this entire time? And now I wonder what else you're keeping from me. I can't trust you."

"Yes, you can."

She shook her head. "I need you to leave."

"I'm not finished. There are some things I need you to look at and answer."

"I don't care." She pointed at the door. "I can't stand the sight of you right now. Get out."

He pulled a paper out of his back pocket and unfolded it. "This is a list of names. I need to know if you recognize them from when your dad was stationed in South Korea."

An incessant ringing filled her ears. "What does that have to do with anything?"

He rubbed his temples. "There was a mission your brother was supposed to help out with the next day. This was a mission that was years in the making. I believe Manny was part of making sure that mission didn't happen, but I don't think he acted alone. And whoever helped had to be someone who knew or knows South Korea well. So, this is a list of everyone involved in that dogfight, both in the air and on the ground—my team included. I need to know if you know any of them."

She grabbed the list. "This is quite long."

"Take your time."

"I don't want you working on this anymore." She dropped her hands to her sides, letting the paper fall to the floor. "I can't trust a fucking word that comes out of your damn mouth."

"Yes. You can. You have to understand that I'm risking—"

"Just get out." She stormed across the room and yanked open the door. "Don't worry. I won't jeopardize your career." She pointed. "Now please leave."

"Priela. You're being unreasonable."

"I don't care about the details of the mission. I get you couldn't tell me that. But you could have mentioned that you were there." She poked him in the chest. "Keeping that from me is like me faking a pregnancy."

"That's not a fair comparison."

"That's how I feel. Please don't make me ask you again."

"I'm not letting this go." He stood in the doorway. "I'm going to get to the bottom of what happened, so please look at the list and let me know." He turned. "Oh. And because I want you to know you can trust me, and I don't want to be accused of lying again, I'm going to be meeting with your father tomorrow. I'll be giving him that list as well."

"You're an arrogant, controlling asshole." She gave him a little push. Not too hard, but enough to encourage him out the door, which she slammed shut and locked behind him. Turning her back, she leaned against the wood and let her butt slide to the floor. She curled her knees to her chest and hugged them tightly. The tears came hot and fast.

She desperately wanted the world to know that her brother loved his country. That he would never do anything to endanger the safety of his team or national security. More importantly, she wanted the Navy, something that had been a huge part of their lives, to acknowledge that her brother was a true hero.

If she were totally honest, she could admit that she'd loved her time in the service and there had been moments she'd considered re-enlisting. If the Navy had a place for a culinary chef, she might have considered it. She'd even thought about the reserves, but she needed to chase her dreams, and her father helped her make that final decision—and supported it.

So had Isaac.

The last time she'd spoken to him, he'd been

worried about an upcoming mission and how dangerous it could be for the men on the ground. She had some understanding of what that meant.

She crawled across the kitchen floor and grabbed the piece of paper Troy had left. Her fingers twitched. She recognized a few names, but those were the men who were on her brother's team, and one was a friend of her father's. No one so far that she knew from when her father had been stationed in South Korea.

Until she came to two names.

Samuel Weston and Waylon King.

She'd met them when she'd been in high school in South Korea. Weston had been under her father's command and had been a royal pain in the ass. He was arrogant and cocky, and her father couldn't wait to have him transferred. But Weston wanted nothing to do with that. He loved being in South Korea, and he'd begged her father to let him stay.

And wherever Sam went, King followed.

But Isaac hadn't told her that they were anywhere near him before he died, and she figured that would have been a conversation since Isaac and Sam had had words on more than one occasion and her brother didn't trust Sam.

She wiped away her tears and stood. No way did she want to call Troy. But she knew him well enough to know that he would continue trying to find the truth behind her brother's death. He was his job. She found her cell. "Hey, Siri. Call Troy Bowie."

It rang once. "Priela? Are you okay?" he asked.

"I'm angry as hell at you and I don't forgive you," she said. "But I recognized a couple of names." She padded across the kitchen and placed a mug under her Keurig to make a cup of cocoa. "Both were stationed in South Korea under my father's command."

"That's interesting," he said.

The sound of a car echoed through the cell.

"Are you in the ferry line?"

"No. I'm sitting on your steps," he said. "Well, now I'm standing at your door."

She held the mug to her lips and turned.

He waved and gave a little smile. "I needed a few minutes to pull myself together before I got on my Harley and drove away." He pressed his head against the windowpane like a pathetic puppy.

"Don't take this gesture as forgiveness." She set the phone on the counter and opened the door. "Why didn't you leave?"

"I wasn't in any condition to drive," he said.

"The ferry is right there."

"But with the way I was feeling, I would have taken the road up to deception pass, and I would have pushed the bike's limits, and that would have been dangerous. I'm a lot of things, but I'm not stupid or crazy. So, I figured I'd just sit there until my emotions calmed down."

"Do you want some hot chocolate?" She shouldn't offer him anything but a kick in the ass, but she didn't have any fight left.

And she still wanted answers.

"Yes, please." He leaned against the counter. "I'm sorry I didn't tell you sooner. I've been agonizing over this ever since you asked me to help you."

"I can't change what you did and I'm too tired to fight with you about it." She handed him a mug. "But I do want to talk to you about my father."

He nodded. "First, can you tell me about the names you recognized?"

"It goes hand in hand with my dad." She blew out a puff of air. "Let's go sit in the family room." She didn't wait for him to answer before scurrying off to put her feet up in her favorite chair.

He kept his distance and sat in the recliner across the room.

Smart man.

"Okay, so the two men I recognized are Samuel Weston and Waylon King."

Troy set his mug on the table next to his chair and leaned forward. "Did you know them well?"

"No. But my dad did, and he didn't like Weston. He was kind of an arrogant prick."

"I've heard that." Troy rubbed his temple. "As I said, I'm meeting your father tomorrow. Do you want to come?"

She dropped her mug and spilled her hot chocolate all over her lap. "Fuck," she muttered, moving to the edge of the leather furniture, thankful none of the chocolatey drink had gone anywhere but on her clothing. "Are you kidding me?"

"No." He jumped to his feet and raced into the kitchen. He returned with a roll of paper towels and started to clean up her lap. "You don't want to be kept in the dark, and I don't want to lie to you anymore."

She appreciated Troy's gesture and was thankful he wanted to be honest with her, but she worried about how much he was putting his career on the line, and how selfish she'd become about that. It wasn't right.

"Let me go get you some dry pants." He took off up the stairs.

She dropped her head back and stared at the ceiling fan, which desperately needed to be dusted. Now that she'd taken a few moments to digest everything that Troy had told her, she understood the gravity of what Troy was doing for her, and she had no right to be this mad. Looking into it was one thing. He'd been tasked with that before he'd met her, so it wasn't a giant leap for him to be asking for more information.

Telling her about it, or going to see her father—well, that could be considered treason and she didn't want him to not only end his career, but ruin his life so she could clear her brother's name.

"Here you go." He held up a towel, a pair of leggings, and a fresh pair of underwear.

She smiled. "Thanks." She shed her wet clothes right there and put on the dry ones.

He turned.

Which made her laugh, but she appreciated him being a gentleman.

He took her dirty clothes and tossed them into the hamper by the laundry room. "Why don't you want to come?" He made himself comfortable on the edge of her chair, resting his hand on her calf. "I'm sure your parents would love to see you."

"My father won't speak freely with you if I'm there," she admitted. "I'm no longer enlisted, and I was never going to make a career out of the military. He'll respect your rank. And you probably have a higher security clearance than he ever had. He'll tell you whatever he can since you're still active."

"And if I want you to come with me?"

"You're only saying that because of our fight."

"That's only partially true, but you had every right to be upset with me, and I don't want to keep things from you. I care too much about you."

She swallowed. Hard. The only reason she'd become so angry was because she'd allowed herself to fall for Troy. Her feelings for him were more intense than anything she'd ever experienced before with any man. "I was only upset about you being there. Not about keeping top-secret information from me. I don't want you to put your career on the line."

"I already have." He cupped her face. "And I have no regrets. Something isn't right about what happened that day, and since I was there, I've found a way to make sure my poking around won't get me into trouble."

"You've mentioned that." She curled her fingers around his wrists and gently tugged. She just wasn't ready for the intimate contact.

"While watching the video with you, I've figured out a way to push even harder. You see, me and my wingman were the first members of my team to arrive. I fired at the enemy just as they were bugging out. We were all debriefed in different places, and when I was tasked to document Isaac's tactical maneuvers, it was for a specific reason, and that's all I focused on."

"Has anyone ever told you that you take forever to get to the point when you're talking shop?"

"It pisses my commander off." He laughed. "Point is, I know I'm one of the best pilots, but I don't need a pat on the back, and I sure as shit don't need to watch myself. So I didn't. But when I pointed my plane out to you, I noticed how Manny and the enemy interacted, and it's not right. In the heat of the moment, no one would see it, and even looking at the footage, it all happens so fast, that even most experts might miss it at first glance. Until one point. And that's when Manny doesn't fire."

"He could have choked."

"That's possible. However, Manny would have been shot down, but the enemy didn't fire either and based on position, he had to have had tone, maybe even lock. Not to mention Manny wasn't the kind of fighter pilot who got flustered. I had to study everyone's flying habits before I watched his specific encounter so I could understand how each pilot reacted under pressure. He'd been in a couple of dicey situations before, so I don't buy it," Troy said. "Between Manny hanging back, saying Isaac ordered him to do so—when no one else heard Isaac say that—the broken comms, and the way he handled his jet during the dogfight, I think Manny was working with the enemy. But he wasn't alone."

"Manny met Weston in South Korea when he and my brother came to visit when I was in high school."

"Did they all get along?"

"Not really. Weston was a dick and had words with my dad in front of my brother. That never goes over well. I only remember because when Weston left the house, he called me little girl." She shivered. "I always hated shit like that."

"I can imagine," Troy said.

"Isaac wasn't thrilled to be working with him or King, but what was he going to do?"

"Not much," Troy said. "You mentioned your brother was paranoid. Did he talk to anyone besides you about it?"

"He probably talked to my dad. They were close. More like brothers as Isaac got older." She rested her hand on his leg. "There was one more name on that list that jumped out at me, but not so much from being in South Korea. Someone who was and still is a good friend of my father's."

"And who's that?"

"Commander Ross Bosen."

Troy's jaw dropped open. He took her hand and squeezed. "How does he know Commander Bosen?"

"I've known Ross my entire life."

"You're on a first-name basis with my commander?" Troy asked.

"Ross is your commander?"

"Not for much longer. Once I transfer to Virginia and the Special Tactical Squadron with Delta Force, I'll have a new commander." Troy nodded. "But please tell me how you know him so well."

"He's like a brother to my dad. They went to the academy together and were in each other's weddings. I grew up calling him Uncle Ross."

"This just got complicated," Troy said. "If my commander finds out I'm meeting with your dad tomorrow before I have a chance to do all this through proper channels, I'm fucked."

"My dad won't do that to you. He might be a rules man, but he'll hear you out before he tosses you under the bus."

"I hope you're right." He glanced at his watch. "Shit. I just missed the last ferry."

She palmed his cheek. "You can stay here tonight."

"I have to get up early. My buddy is flying out of the small airport on Whidbey. I don't want to disturb you any more than I already have this evening."

"Would you feel better if I told you that I forgive you?"

He let out a short laugh. "Maybe." His smoldering gaze held hers hostage.

She couldn't look away if she tried. She was in deep, and there was no way she would climb out without leaving her heart behind. It was time to give in to her emotions.

It was time to finally take a risk, and Troy was a man worth putting her love on the line for.

Troy had never been nervous about taking a woman to bed before. He didn't suffer from the fear of rejection because, when it happened—and it did—he brushed it off and moved on. He knew he wasn't for everyone. He might be cocky in the air, and he didn't think he was all that bad to look at, but he wasn't so arrogant as to believe that all women found him attractive. Besides, he wasn't searching for lasting love. He only wanted to be in the moment. Enjoy a good time with someone who didn't have any expectations.

But with Priela, he found himself in a world he'd been avoiding. Since he'd met her, she'd been the center of his universe. She was the first thing he thought about when he woke up, and the last thing on his mind when he drifted off to sleep. He could tell himself that it was all because of her brother and how he'd dove into the investigation, but he'd be lying to himself.

While it was important to Troy to find out what really happened the day Isaac died, and while Priela had become part of the air Troy breathed, the thought of her not being in his life sucked the oxygen right out of his lungs.

He laid her in the bed, kissing her sweet lips. His hands roamed her body, gently massaging her soft but firm muscles. She gave herself so freely, and it humbled him. He wanted to please her so badly, he no longer cared about himself. All that mattered was her pleasure, but she seemed to have different plans when she rolled him to his back and took him into her mouth.

He stared at her as she lapped at him, using her tongue and hands at the same time, squeezing and caressing until his breathing came in short, erratic pants. He scooped up her blond hair and piled it on top of her head, tugging gently. "Priela. I need you to stop."

She wiped her lips and smiled.

He groaned. "You're killing me."

"I hope not literally."

"Close." He stood at the edge of the bed, turning her around so she was on all fours. He placed his hand over her round bottom, gliding it up her spine, across her shoulders, and around to her breasts. He tugged and pinched at her nipples. He slipped a couple of fingers inside her, and she clenched around him, moaning. Gently, he guided himself inside her, keeping the pace slow and controlled at first. Reaching around her waist, he found her hard nub. Thrusting deep and hard, he brought her orgasm to the surface, making her shiver with delight.

He loved how his name rolled off her tongue in the heat of passion. He let his climax spill from his body into hers in a powerful surge.

They collapsed on the bed, wrapping their arms and legs around each other, gasping for breath.

"I think I'm falling for you," he whispered, tucking them in under the covers. "I care for you in ways that scare me."

She snuggled into his chest. "I'm terrified about my feelings."

"We've gotten ourselves into a situation, haven't we?" He kissed her temple.

"I'd say so."

"What are we going to do about it?" he asked.

She tilted her head. Her soft eyes caught the light filtering through the window. "I believe I'm too far gone to be saved."

He brushed her hair from her face. "Do you really need to be saved from me?"

She smiled. "We're crazy if we think this can ever work."

"Maybe we're nuts to think it won't."

11

Priela set a cup of coffee in front of Troy. "If Reid is going with you, then text him to bring all that food I made. It's in his fridge." She wished she could say that she didn't have reservations about him flying off to meet with her father, but by the way her stomach twisted and churned, it weighed heavily on her mind and wasn't going away until the meeting had concluded.

It wasn't that she was concerned about Troy coming face-to-face with her dad. She didn't care if her dad knew that she and Troy were in some kind of relationship, even if they didn't know what they were doing or what would happen moving forward. Her only concern was how the commander would react to Troy's information, and would her dad change his tune when it came to accepting whatever the Navy's report said?

"He already knows." Troy stuffed his face with another bite of the French toast she'd made him for breakfast. "I thought you said you weren't like a pastry chef or something?"

"I'm not. But breakfast foods aren't that hard."

"Tell that to Ziggy. She can't cook shit," Troy said. He wiped his mouth before taking a sip of coffee. "She can't even boil water."

"And are you a good cook?"

He laughed. "I know how to make shit on a shingle. That's about it."

"Aren't you a good Navy boy?" She reached across the table and took a slice of crispy bacon, breaking off a piece. "All of a sudden, you look so serious."

"We need to talk before I leave."

"I don't like it when you say that or when you use that tone. It reminds me of when I got called to the principal's office." She leaned back in her chair and sipped her tea. She might not have known Troy for very long, but she felt as though she knew him better than some of her lifelong friends. Based on how he fiddled with his fork and pushed at his food, something troubled him.

"This is kind of serious." He pushed his plate aside. "And I don't want to wait to bring it up. I'm kind of surprised you didn't notice last night."

"Notice what?"

"I didn't use protection." He arched a brow. "We've never talked about birth control, other than us using a condom the first night we were together. Outside of that, I have no idea if you are on the pill or anything else."

Her heart dropped to her gut. She'd gone off the pill four months ago because she always forgot to take it. And since she had no reason at the time, she just never went about getting any kind of replacement. If she found herself with a man, condoms were always the best choice anyway, considering she would make them use one for other reasons.

"Well, shit," she said. "That is a problem."

"So, I take it that means we just played Russian roulette."

"Your assumption would be correct." She blew out a puff of air. "I can't believe I was so careless. Even when I was on the pill, I always made any man I was with use a condom."

"I'm not just any man, and I don't ever want to hear about other guys again."

She cocked her head. "Are you jealous?"

"Hell, yes," he said. "But I have to admit, that was the first time since my early twenties that I've forgotten to use one."

"After what Daisy did to you, I'm not surprised." She kept his gaze. "I wouldn't trap you."

"What scares me is that I don't think I'd feel that way if you were pregnant."

She coughed. "That word does freak me out."

"I can't say it rolled off my tongue easily, but I meant what I said. I'm not afraid of it."

"I have to be honest. I am." She reached across the table, sliding his plate in her direction. She stabbed her fork into the last few pieces of the tasty breakfast that he hadn't finished. Normally, she didn't eat like this, but her nerves had gotten the better of her. She also took the time to mentally count the days from her last period.

That didn't make her feel any better.

"That coming from the one who said she wanted to have children."

"Maybe in like five years or something," she said. "And, come on, you and I having a kid wouldn't be a good idea. Let's be realistic about things."

He nodded. "Right now, I agree. We're just

getting to know each other. But down the road? I can see it."

She choked on a piece of French toast. She pounded on her chest before reaching for her mug and taking a few sips of her tea. "What the hell did you just say?"

"I have no idea." He shook his head. "You've turned my world upside down, and I find myself wanting things I thought I could live without." He reached across the table and took her hands. "I have to fly back to Hawaii in nine days, where I'll pack up my things and move to Virginia. I have no idea how long I'll be stationed there. I've honestly been trying to get a run at a base here in Seattle."

"But being Delta Force, you'll be deployed all over the world."

"Not for long stints and not necessarily with my position. I love flying, and I didn't ever think I'd give up being a fighter pilot, but when Delta Force came knocking, I knew it was an opportunity I couldn't refuse. I get to fly and will still have the chance to go on missions. It will be different, though. I'm working intelligence. Setting up search and rescue. Dealing with all branches of the military and the government. Running training exercises and working with the best of the best. It's an honor."

"Troy, what are you getting at?" Priela stared into his caring eyes, wishing she could turn away.

"Virginia could be anywhere from a three- to ten-year station. I don't know, but I have made my intention clear that I want to end up in Seattle at some point. That was a promise Delta Force made me when I signed the paperwork."

"Are you saying that you're going to end up here?"

"Not for a few years and long distance would totally suck, but I'm willing to try, unless you want to fly with me to Virginia. Check it out and see if it's a place you'd like to make a go at a catering business for a few years."

Her jaw slackened. "I've known you for a week, and you're asking me to move across the country with you?"

"Yes and no. I'm asking you to come and visit me on a regular basis and think about it. I'll come here as much as I can." He stood and strolled to the other side of the table, helping her to her feet. He cupped her cheeks. "I want to make a real go of this. It won't be easy with my career, and the distance won't help. But I'm willing to do whatever I can to make it work. Are you?"

"Wow. You certainly know how to make a girl speechless." She rested her hands on his shoulders. "You need to go catch the ferry so you don't miss your flight."

"You're avoiding my question."

"I am." She rose on tiptoe and gave him a quick but passionate kiss. "We'll discuss this again when you return."

"I'll call you after I speak to your dad." He headed toward the door. Glancing over his shoulder, he smiled. "I'll be thinking about you all day."

"No, you won't."

"Oh, yes, I will." He winked. "I'll see you tonight." He stepped outside, gently closing the door.

She flattened her hands over her stomach, which had filled with butterflies. Besides being concerned that she could be pregnant—which scared the crap out of her—she couldn't believe she was considering moving to Virginia. She'd lost her mind.

And her heart.

Troy stretched out his arm and shook Decker Griggs' hand. "It's a pleasure to meet you."

"Likewise." Decker was over six feet tall. His body was thick and his hair still standard miliary style. "Good to see you again, Reid."

"You, too," Reid said.

"The bird is all gassed up and ready to go." Dustin strolled across the pavement.

"Great. Let's get the show on the road." Decker waved his hand toward the stairs. "We can talk business on the ride."

Troy wasn't sure how much he wanted to fill Decker in on at this point. Too many cooks and all. But both Dustin and Reid had agreed that Decker knew things and that Troy should at least drop a few names and pick the man's brain.

He settled into one of the seats and buckled in. It was always strange to be a passenger, and Troy didn't like it. He'd rather be in the cockpit with Dustin. Maybe on the way home, Dustin would let him fly.

"How's your wife?" Decker asked.

"Darcie's great." Reid nodded. "I think I mentioned that Troy is her brother."

"You did," Decker said. "And both you and Dustin said he had some questions for me."

Troy cleared his throat. "Do you mind if I dive right in?"

"My all means." Decker nodded.

"Have you ever heard of a mission called *Pins and Needles?*" Troy asked.

"Why?" Decker folded his arms across his chest.

"I was in the Sea of Japan the day before it was supposed to go down. An incident happened, and a good man died."

"I might have heard about that," Decker said. "But I don't know the details."

"I believe that one of the fighter pilots flying that day tipped off the enemy and not only caused the incident, but also prevented *Operation Pins and Needles* from happening."

"What is it you're looking for?" Decker asked.

"Proof that three Navy men were working with the North Koreans." Troy pulled out a piece of paper and handed it to Decker. "Manny's dead. He supposedly killed himself, but his death was originally—"

"He was murdered," Decker said matter-of-factly.

"How do you know?"

"Because I read the file, and the doctor who performed the autopsy had no choice but to rule it a suicide. But if you read the notes, it's a suspicious death; he just couldn't prove it, and the family wanted the case closed." Decker held up the paper. "Who are the other two names?"

Troy had a billion questions regarding how and why Trib knew all that but decided not to get sidetracked. "They were on the ground and had firsthand knowledge of the mission. They are actually working a similar mission the Navy will try to execute sometime in the near future. I fear they will do their best to make sure it doesn't happen."

"And you want me to find out if that's true?"

"I'm working on the old case. I'd like you to see what these two are up to now before they head back to South Korea. Currently, they're in Pensacola."

"I can do that. And I can help with the cold case," Decker said. "Might as well have more than one set of eyes."

Troy couldn't argue that point. "I can't be involved with my active-duty status."

"Understood. I'll report back to Reid and Dustin."

"I appreciate that."

Decker took out his phone and tapped on the screen. "Hey. I need a team on two guys by the names of Samuel Weston and Waylon King. They are stationed in Pensacola. Nick Sarich is there on a different mission. See if one of his brothers or his mom's husband is available and put them both on this. The targets have high security clearance, so we need to get people on the inside. Mia can help with that. I need to know what they are working on, who they are talking to, emails—personal and work—and, most importantly, I want to know if they are traitors. Got it?" Decker nodded. "Good." He set his cell on his lap. "I've got people everywhere. If they are up to no good, I'll know it soon. Now, knowing and doing something about it are two different things, as I'm sure you've figured out in your career."

"I have."

"If you ever decide to leave the military and go private. I can use good men like you. I've got two offices in Florida and I'm open to starting another anywhere in the US. Name it."

"Thanks, but for now, I'm happy right where I am."

"Can't blame a guy for trying, especially when I can get a lot more done this way, bending and breaking the rules and playing nice."

Troy didn't know about that, but he wasn't about to argue with Decker. He didn't think that would go over too well. He leaned back in his seat, looking out the window.

"Can I ask you something?" Decker asked.

"Sure," Troy said.

"Why is this so important to you?"

"My girlfriend's brother was the man who died that day, and he was held responsible for the incident. When in reality, someone set him up to take the fall. I want to make sure his name is cleared for her and her family's sake." Troy glanced toward Reid, who cracked a smile. Most likely over his use of the word *girlfriend*.

"That's a noble reason," Decker said. "Now, if you don't mind, I need a nap. I flew commercial from Florida to here, and it sucked."

"Sounds good to me." Troy closed his eyes. Immediately, an image of Priela came into his mind. She stood on her porch with her blond hair blowing in the breeze as she sipped a glass of wine. He'd do anything for Priela.

Anything.

A thought that both terrified and invigorated him.

Troy paced in front of the restaurant where Commander Sloane had asked him to meet. He'd gone inside twice, and the commander had yet to arrive. Of course, Troy had been early.

A dark SUV pulled into the parking lot. That had to be the commander.

Troy's pulse kicked up a notch.

The driver's door opened, and Priela's father stepped onto the pavement. Then the passenger-side door opened, and Commander Ross Bosen appeared.

Fuck. Troy hadn't expected that. Mentally, he went over every detail of his conversation with Commander Sloane. He told himself it wasn't that bad. That he hadn't just shot himself in the foot.

"Hello, Troy," his commander said with a tilt of his head and an all-knowing look.

Shit.

"Commander Bosen. What are you doing here?" he asked with his heart in his throat.

"I should be asking you that." Boson waved his hand in a dismissive gesture. "I don't think you've met my old friend, Ben Sloane."

"I have not." Troy stretched out his arm. "Thanks for taking the time out of your day. I appreciate it."

"Let's walk over to the park," Bosen said. "I'm not comfortable talking in the diner."

Troy swallowed the growing lump, but it didn't go down easily. For the first time in his career, he had no idea how to handle a situation. He'd always acted in pure adrenaline and instinct. He trusted his skills both in the air and on the ground. He wasn't cocky. He was confident because he'd trained his entire life for this job. He took it seriously. He paid attention in the classroom, and he never took unnecessary risks.

Okay. That wasn't entirely true. He liked his flybys, but outside of that, he was a good sailor and right now, he was at a total loss. He squared his shoulders. "I don't know what Commander Sloane has told you."

"You can call me Ben," Priela's father said. "I'd prefer it, so please don't revert back to the commander or sir shit."

Troy nodded.

"For the record, Ben has filled me in on everything." Commander Bosen waved to a picnic table in the center of the park. It wasn't crowded, so they should be able to speak freely.

Not that Troy wanted to at this point.

"I knew that I was sharing you with Delta Force

for the next month, but I hadn't realized your new commander in Virginia had given you Isaac's flight to study. That came as a bit of a shock to me," Commander Bosen said. "When Ben called, I was surprised to hear your name. I've never known you to break rank."

Troy ran a hand over his jaw. He had no idea how to play this, except to be honest. It was his only hope to help clear Isaac's name and save his own ass. "I meant no disrespect to you, or my commander in Delta Force," Troy began. "However, I don't think what happened the day Isaac died was an accident. Between what I experienced myself that day, studying the footage, and discovering a few things about some people involved, something is terribly wrong and all I'm trying to do is find the truth, nothing more. For the record, I'm mostly going through proper channels since my job was to break down the dogfight and use it for future reference. When doing that, we often find unexpected things. I've requested more detailed information of the missions involved."

"Can you prove anything you've found out so far?" Ben asked.

"I'm close," Troy said.

"How close?" Commander Bosen asked.

Not close enough. "I have people working on getting proof," Troy said. "I wouldn't be doing this if I didn't believe that something went very wrong that day." He rolled his neck. "Do I have permission to speak freely?"

"Son, we might outrank you, but you have high security clearance and at the end of the day, know more than we do, so please," Ben said.

Troy blew out a puff of air. "If you watch the video I have, you'll see how Manny doesn't engage when he should. They originally ruled his death as suspicious, and two men who were once under your command were on the ground in South Korea. Samuel Weston and Waylon King. They were part of *Operation Pins and Needles,* and both are currently working on a similar mission. I would bet good money that mission also fails because the North Koreans are given information about it. Because that's the only way they could have known exactly when Isaac would be flying and that Manny would hang back when their comms were down."

"Take a breath, son," Ben said. "You got all that from watching one film of my son flying?"

"There was a little more to it. But yes."

Ben and Commander Bosen exchanged glances.

"You've done what we've been trying to do for

two years," Commander Bosen said. "I can't believe that Weston and King are involved in this, but I'm not shocked."

"Excuse me?" Troy asked.

"We had no idea who was in charge of that mission," Ben said. "I was retiring, and Bosen doesn't have the security clearance. And he wasn't in charge of any teams out there."

"But we were there," Troy said. "*I* was there and he's my commander."

"Our ship was on her way home," Commander Bosen said. "It was a fluke that they called us in. But no matter how much I tried to get information on what happened, I was blocked at every turn. I only knew what Ben told me, given what his son had said before the mission, but we didn't even know about *Pins and Needles* until about a month ago. That was highly classified. I'm shocked you know about it."

"I was told when they gave me the footage. It's also exactly the kind of thing I'll be working on with the Special Tactical Squadron with Delta Force." Troy rubbed his jaw. "Ben, may I ask you a personal question?"

"Sure."

"You've been trying to clear your son's name all this time?"

"I have," Ben said.

"Why have you let Priela believe otherwise?"

"When Isaac first died, she wouldn't let it go, and I was afraid she'd piss off the wrong people and get herself in trouble. I got her into whatever cooking school she wanted and helped her focus her attention on that, hoping she'd let it go. But since you're here, I guess she never did."

"Nope. But until me, she hadn't found anyone with the resources to find the truth, and I've hired the Aegis Network, which is run by ex-military, to help me with some information that I can't get on my own."

"My turn to ask a personal question," Ben said. "Why would you do that? What is my daughter to you?" he asked with a tight jaw.

"The simplest answer is that she's my girlfriend."

"I see," Ben said. "Do you love her?"

Troy swallowed. When he opened his mouth, he wanted to lie because admitting it made it real. "I do."

Ben laughed. "I'm sorry. It's not that I find that

funny, but my daughter swore to me that she'd never fall for a military man."

"I never said she loved me back," Troy said quietly. "It's complicated and truth be told, I've never said the words out loud."

Ben arched a brow. "Well, I hope you find a way to uncomplicate it. I think I like you."

"Thank you, sir. I appreciate that vote of confidence." He glanced at his watch. "Unfortunately, I have a flight to catch. I'll be in touch."

"Troy," Commander Bosen said, "you didn't see me today, and I didn't see you."

"Thank you, sir."

"Your point of contact for this is Ben. Not me. Got it?"

"I do." Troy stood.

"I'm going to miss being your commander. Delta Force is lucky to have you." Commander Bosen slapped him on the back. "You're a good sailor and even more importantly, you're a good man. You will always have a glowing recommendation from me wherever you go."

"That means the world to me," Troy said.

"Give my daughter a hug for me, and when you can, bring her back to see her parents. We miss her."

"Will do." He jogged across the street with his heart pounding like crazy. He couldn't wait to get back to Seattle and share this conversation with Priela.

He wanted to share everything with her, and that no longer scared him.

12

"Thank you so much for coming over." Priela sipped the crisp white wine. Normally, she didn't drink during the day, but nothing about today was normal. Between Troy's declarations and worrying about possibly being pregnant, Priela couldn't concentrate on anything. So, when Darcie called, asking if she had any plans, Priela had jumped at the chance to get her mind off everything.

Well, her mind was still hyper-focused on Troy meeting with her father, but at least she could talk to someone instead of going crazy with her thoughts.

"My pleasure," Darcie said. "Besides, I'm not used to having my husband gone. It's usually the other way around."

"He doesn't travel at all?"

"He does some, but he tries to schedule his trips when I'm gone. Not to mention he was able to get a manufacturer right here in Seattle, so he's traveling less and less. He tries to get people to come to him if he can, especially now that we are entering the final countdown for this baby." Darcie lifted her croissant sandwich and took a large bite. "Oh, my God. This is amazing."

"The baked goods come from Crystal's bakery."

"You two make for a great team."

"I use her for a lot of things," Priela admitted. If she moved to Virginia, she'd lose that contact, but there were bakeries everywhere. My God, she was really considering moving with a man she'd just met. She needed to slow down. They could do the long-distance thing for a little while.

Shit. It was coast to coast with a military man.

That was a recipe for disaster.

"Do you mind if I ask you a personal question?" Priela asked.

"Not at all."

"Was it really only a couple of weeks that the two of you were together before you got pregnant?"

"Yes," Darcie said. "But we'd been together for

a couple of years and then broke up for a year. So, it wasn't like we were total strangers."

"And you have no regrets?"

"Oh. I have one," Darcie said with a laugh. "During our breakup, I slept with one of my captains. That was a big mistake, and Reid likes to tease me about it every once in a while."

"Did Reid know him?"

"Oh, boy, did he. And a few months ago, Captain Jim nearly had us killed, but that's all behind us. Jim's in jail, and we have a little one on the way." She patted her belly. "I'm shocked I'm so excited about having a baby. This was not something I had planned for this young, but Reid is older than I, so he's thrilled, and he'd like to have a second one close in age, which makes sense. He doesn't want to be an old man when his kids graduate high school."

"You and Reid will make great parents."

"Thanks. I know Reid will be an awesome father, but I'm not so sure about how I will fare with the parenting. It wasn't high on my priority list of things to do. Callie keeps telling me that it will come naturally."

"It will."

"Speaking of kids. How did my brother really do with babysitting? I've gotten mixed reviews."

Priela smiled. "He did better than I thought he would, though he didn't handle a messy diaper that well, tried to give her a bath in the kitchen sink, and ended up giving himself one as well. It was pretty funny."

"I would have liked to have seen that."

Priela took out her cell. "I happen to have documented it."

"That's classic." Darcie swiped her finger across the phone. "Troy is such a goof. He's a cross between serious and a con-artist, which is hard to do. Growing up, he almost never got in trouble at school. He was more of a rule follower than a rule breaker, except every once in a while, he'd do something so outrageous we'd all be standing there like, what the heck? And he'd get away with whatever it was because it was unexpected."

"He's a good man." Priela sighed.

"You really like him, don't you?"

"Is it that obvious?" She tossed her napkin onto the plate. "I hadn't meant for this to happen."

"No one ever does."

"It's happening too fast. My head is spinning."

Priela needed to talk with someone about what she and Troy had talked about, and she didn't have too many girlfriends. Truth be told, she had none. There weren't a lot of women at the naval academy and even less on a battleship. Trusting women had been difficult as well.

Darcie had always been friendly, and they'd gone out to lunch before, so she felt comfortable discussing personal things with her. But this was about her brother, which made it awkward. "Before Reid, had you ever been in love?"

"Nope," Darcie said. "What about you?"

"I've never loved anyone."

"Are you in love with my brother?"

"I don't know. I mean, is it possible to fall in love that quickly?"

"I believe it is," Darcie said. "Have you said those words to Troy?"

Priela shook her head. "But he mentioned me going to Virginia with him."

"He did what?" Darcie's eyes grew so wide they looked like those drawings from that famous artist. "I don't mean to sound so shocked, but Troy is love and commitment-phobic thanks to his ex, Ginny."

"I know. I've heard all about that, and I know what Daisy did to him, so I was as shocked as you are when he brought it up this morning like it was no big deal." Priela inhaled sharply and let it out slowly. "Not to mention, we made one huge mistake and didn't use birth control last night."

Darcie dropped her head to the table and groaned. "Troy's in love. I never thought I'd see the day, but he absolutely loves you."

"Is that a bad thing?"

"Oh, God, no." Darcie popped her head up. "We all figured if and when it happened, he'd fall like a ton of bricks. And we were all hoping it would be with you. It's just faster than he flies a plane and he's always so against getting married and having kids."

"Tell me about it," Priela said. "Please don't take this the wrong way, but I don't want to be pregnant. Not yet. I need more time to get to know him."

"I can understand that." Darcie nodded.

Bang!

"What the hell was that?" Priela jumped up from the table. She inched her way toward the front of the house when the door swung open and two men with guns barreled into her home.

Darcie gasped.

Priela backed up, knocking over one of the chairs.

"Hello, Priela. It's been a long time." Weston stuck a gun in her face.

She reached behind her, grabbing Darcie by the hand. "What are you doing here?"

King closed the door and locked it. "Your boyfriend opened a can of worms that has put us in a difficult situation, so we're going to have to clean up that mess. Unfortunately, that means some people have to die."

Troy sprawled out on one of the benches in the back of the private jet and closed his eyes. He'd texted Priela, letting her know that the meeting had gone well and that he'd fill her in with all the details when he got home.

Home.

What did that mean?

And what would it look like in the future?

Was he asking too much of her to move to Virginia? Should he consider joining an organization like the special operations company that Decker owned? There were a lot of options. He didn't have to be so demanding about his career. Of course, he had three years left in his current contract, so there was that. And he would have to honor it, but he had choices, and if he wanted Priela in his life forever, he needed to include her in those decisions.

He chuckled.

How had his life changed so drastically in a week?

"What's so funny over there?" Reid asked.

"I'm in love," Troy said, cracking open one eye.

Reid lowered the paper and tilted his head. "Stranger things have happened."

"Shit," Decker said. "I hate to break up the lovefest, but I've got some bad news."

"What's that?" Troy pushed himself to a seated position.

"I just got intel that your boys, Weston and King, are in Seattle."

"What the fuck?" Troy yanked his cell from his back pocket and found Priela's contact information while staring at Reid. "Come on. Answer the damn phone."

"Hello," a male voice said.

Troy's heart dropped to his gut. "Who is this?"

"The man who's going to kill you."

"Where's Priela?" He undid his buckle and leaned forward.

"For now, she's safe. But if I were you, I'd get back here as soon as possible. Make sure you come alone. We'll be waiting."

Reid signaled that they were a half hour from touchdown.

"I'll be there in an hour," he said. "Let me talk to her."

"Sure thing," the man said.

"Troy?" Priela's voice was shaky and weak.

"Are you hurt?"

"No," she said. "But, Troy, I'm not alone," she whispered. "Darcie was here when they broke in. They have us both."

"We're on our way. Just sit tight and take care of each other. Okay?"

The line went dead.

"Motherfucker," Reid said under his breath. "Dustin, fly this bird faster, or I'm going to jump."

"I'll get Jag, Kyle, and Matt on the horn. I'll make sure someone has eyes on the girls," Troy said.

Reid nodded.

"Count me in," Decker said. "This way you can see what the Aegis Network is made of." Decker smiled. "In case you ever change your mind."

"Thanks." Troy shook out his hands. "We've got

thirty minutes to lay out a plan. Let's make it a good one."

Priela wiggled her hands, but the restraints were too tight. "How are you doing?" she whispered.

"I'm pissed off," Darcie said.

Weston and King were in the family room, watching television of all things, while Priela and Darcie sat on the kitchen floor.

About every ten minutes, either Weston or King got up and made their way around the house. They were due to make their rounds in about three minutes.

"This is the second time in a year I've been tied up, and not by my husband." Darcie shifted. "He's not going to take too kindly to this."

"They should be here in about eight minutes if my calculations are correct."

"I suspect Jag and Matt are lurking around somewhere," Darcie whispered.

"I'm sorry you got caught up in this." Priela let out a long breath. "Had I not asked your brother to look into Isaac's death, Weston and King wouldn't be in my family room right now."

"This isn't your fault, so don't think twice about it."

"At least we know they'll be outnumbered." Priela hoped that statement was true. She'd hate for this to be an ambush. She closed her eyes. That was a horrible thought.

A tap on the front door caught her attention. She gasped.

Weston stomped through the house. He held his weapon high as he approached the entrance. "Looks like your boyfriend is here." He pulled open the door. "King. Check the outside."

"On it," King said.

"You must be Troy," Weston stepped to the side, letting Troy into the kitchen.

Priela locked gazes with him. A tear rolled down her cheek.

"I am," he said. "Why don't you let the girls go since it's me you want?"

"I can't do that," Weston said.

"How about you let Darcie go. She has absolutely nothing to do with this, and she's pregnant."

Weston shook his head. "She's knows too much." He shrugged. "Sorry."

Priela scooted closer to Darcie. She couldn't hold her hand, but she could press her arm against

Darcie's. While Priela believed that Troy would get them out of this alive, they both needed human contact.

"Killing all of us will only bring attention to yourself, ruining your plans," Troy said. He shifted his gaze from Priela back to Weston.

"I don't see how." Weston waved his gun. "Sit down."

Troy did as he was told; there was no point in arguing. "How do you plan on getting away with this?" He needed to keep Weston talking for as long as he could to give his men enough time to take down the three guys they knew Weston and King had brought, as well as King, who had stepped outside.

Hopefully there would be no surprises, but Troy was flying blind at this point. He wouldn't know if they were successful until the cavalry showed up at the door.

"It's pretty simple. We make it look like a break-in and a random act of violence. Three people killed by some crazed lunatic on drugs or something. It happens all the time in Seattle."

"Maybe so. But you're killing a decorated naval captain who was tasked to look into an incident that you might have had something to do with, along with his pregnant sister and his girlfriend, who you've met before. That doesn't sound random. Especially after I just visited Commander Ben Sloane. You remember him, don't you?" Troy shifted his gaze back to Priela. He gave her a weak smile.

She returned the gesture.

So did his sister.

"What does that matter?" Weston asked. "Those are all coincidences that no one really knows about and they won't be linked back to me."

"But isn't that why you're here? To stop me from putting all the pieces of the puzzle together about what happened the day Isaac died?" Troy held up his hand. "Don't answer that because I already have all the answers, and I've already given a report to the Navy that proves you forced Manny into leaving Isaac alone and gave the North Koreans information regarding that flight pattern."

"You don't know what you're talking about."

"Oh, really?" Troy cocked his head. "I know that you sold information about *Operation Pins and Needles* to the North Koreans and that you're still working for them. You're a traitor, and you're going to prison for the rest of your life."

Weston laughed. "You might know that, but there is no way to prove it. Manny is dead, and I covered my tracks. Whatever you think you've uncovered, you don't have all the facts."

Troy smiled. "I was there that day. I saw what happened and I've been studying Isaac's engagement. Manny's account is off and now my superiors, along with the Department of Defense, have my report. The fact you are here and not in Pensacola, where a special investigative team is on their way to question you won't look good for your defense."

"You're bluffing."

Troy shook his head. "Before I came here, I sent everything to my commander with Delta Force. Including the fact that you called me, threatening my girlfriend and my sister. You're fucked." He stood.

"What the fuck are you doing? Sit down, or I'll shoot you."

"No. You won't."

"The fuck I—"

The front door flew open, and two military men wearing full gear stormed the room.

Troy dove toward the girls, covering their bodies in case things went sideways.

Thankfully, they didn't.

"Weston, you're under arrest," one of the men said as they threw Weston to the floor.

"Let me get these things off you." Troy quickly untied Priela and then his sister.

Reid came racing into the room. He knocked Troy over to get to Darcie.

"Jeez, watch it, man."

"Sorry," Reid mumbled. "Darcie. Are you okay?"

"I am now."

Reid lifted his wife and carried her out of the house.

"Hey, you," Troy whispered, brushing Priela's hair from her face. "How are you holding up?"

She wrapped her arms around his shoulders. "I've never been so scared in my life."

"Me either," he said, lifting her into his arms.

"I don't believe that for one second. You were so calm."

"On the outside. Inside, it killed me to see the woman I love tied up and held at gunpoint by a crazy man."

"I'm not sure I'm ready to hear you say that you love me."

"Okay. Well, let me know when you are so I can say it every day."

"You're so weird."

He set her down on the back of Jag's SUV. "Your father laughed at me when I said I loved you."

She jerked her head back. "You told him that?"

He nodded. "I couldn't help myself."

"I'll get there eventually." She cupped his face. "Thank you."

"For what?"

She brushed her mouth against his lips. "Clearing my brother's name," she whispered.

13

"Wow. What a view." Priela had been all over the world, but she'd only been to a few places in the United States, and now she could add Lake Tahoe to that list. "The water looks amazing." She helped lay the red-and-white-checked tablecloth over the wood tabletop.

"I thought you might like it." Troy had been one surprise after the other in the last week since Weston and King had held her at gunpoint. Besides the fact that Troy had barely left her side, he'd shown himself to be one of the most romantic men she'd ever met—but not in an overbearing way. It was more subtle with things like bringing home a book by her favorite author the day it was released, without her even asking for him to stop at the bookstore to get it.

"I can't say anyone has ever flown me by private jet to a lakeside picnic before."

"I just feel bad you had to cook the meal."

"It's only fair since you're the one who flew the plane."

"Yeah, well, I love flying."

"Even when it's not a fighter jet?"

He nodded. "I don't need to be Mach 2 and upside down. I know I can't do that forever. It's one of the reasons I took the opportunity with Delta when it was handed to me."

"Good to know." She leaned across the table, palming his cheek. "For the record, cooking gets me all hot and bothered."

"Oh. I like the sound of that." He brushed his lips over hers in a tender, sweet kiss. She loved being in his arms, and in two days, she would have to say goodbye.

Only she didn't want to. At least, not permanently. She understood that she'd have to move if they were really going to give this relationship a good chance of survival.

"I have something I need to tell you," she said softly.

"That sounds serious."

"It kind of is." She swallowed. When she'd gotten her period this morning, she was both relieved and saddened. The contradicting emotions continued to riffle about her heart and mind. She did want to have children—in the future. Or so she thought. But with Troy, she could actually see beyond tomorrow and she wanted it all with him.

"Whatever's on your mind, you can tell me anything. I'm always here for you."

She smiled, nodding. "I'm not pregnant."

"Oh. I see," he said. "Well. That's a bit of a relief. I think." He ran a hand over his jaw. "I mean. We're just getting to know each other, although I feel like I've known you my entire life."

"You almost seem disappointed that I'm not." She tilted her head.

"I know it's for the best. I was just starting to think it wouldn't have been the worst thing in the world."

Her heart jumped into her throat. Every day for the last week, she'd thought the same thing, and if she were being completely honest, when she found out for sure that she wasn't pregnant, she'd been sad beyond what she thought was normal.

"Does that scare you?" he asked.

"It does, but only because I was thinking the same thing. But we have so many things to work out and discuss, it's overwhelming."

"Why don't we enjoy our dinner for now?" He popped open a bottle of bubbly and poured it into two plastic glasses. "What did you make us?"

She had to appreciate the deflection. But they would have to discuss the dynamics of their relationship going forward sooner rather than later. "Nothing spectacular. Just some good old-fashioned fried chicken, potato salad, homemade chips, and a little treat that Crystal made."

"Sounds perfect." He sat beside her, helping to set up the rest of the food. Everything with him was easy, and they'd fallen into this kind of comfortable courtship that felt natural as well as exciting.

"I can't believe you leave in two days," she said, not able to let it alone.

"I know. It kind of sucks." He took her hand. "You want to talk about this now, don't you?"

She nodded. For the last week, she'd avoided telling him how she really felt. Saying those three little words would change her world even more. But it was time to put her heart on the line and take a risk. "I won't ever ask you to leave the Navy or give up your new post with Delta Force. I know what your career means to you and how hard you've worked to get where you are."

"I wouldn't ask you to give up your dreams, either." He brushed away a piece of hair that had blown in front of her face. "But I've been thinking a lot about my career lately. I have three years left on my contract and I was thinking—"

She covered his mouth. "You can't give up something that has meant so much to you for me."

"You're not the reason." He took her hand and kissed it. "Decker told me that if I ever left the Navy, he'd be happy to hire me and let me open an Aegis Network office anywhere I wanted. My family means the world to me and they live in Seattle. I always said I'd retire there."

"What are you saying?"

"I have to go to Virginia for a minimum of three years and I was hoping you'd come with me. I know I'm asking a lot because you're just getting started here, but we can come back. I'll work for the Aegis Network and you can start up your catering business again."

"You've got it all figured out."

"I understand if you're not ready to move right away."

Her heart pounded. "Do you remember when

you mentioned that you might love me, and I said I wasn't ready to hear it, much less say it?"

The corners of his mouth turned up into a smile. "I not only remember, but I think about it every day. Why?"

"I might be ready."

"*Might be* isn't good enough," he said. "I need *I'm ready*."

The butterflies in her stomach fluttered about, looking for an escape route, but there wasn't one. Their only hope of release was if she allowed herself to feel every ounce of her love for the one man who gave her the freedom to be exactly who she was without judgment. More importantly, he had no desire to change her in any way. "I love you, Troy."

He smiled widely. "I love you back, Priela." He drew her close, kissing her tenderly. "Will you fly away with me to Virginia?"

"I'd fly anywhere with you."

FOUR WEEKS LATER...

Priela smiled as Troy took all the dessert dishes from the coffee table in the family room to the kitchen.

"Your son is quite the gentleman," her mother said as she took the bottle of wine and poured Henrietta and Harold Bowie another glass of wine. "We've enjoyed getting to know him."

"And we adore your daughter," Harold said. "We're sad to see her leave, but thrilled our kids found each other."

Priela laughed. "Sorry. I don't mean any disrespect, but you did kind of push us together." She stared around the house she'd called home for the last eight months, taking in the boxes scattered everywhere. In three days, she was moving across the country to Virginia.

It wasn't a permanent move. Troy was adamant when it was time for them to have a family, he wanted to do it near family and her parents were in California and his in Seattle.

It was crazy that she was even having the conversation. She tried to look at the move as just another adventure, but deep down she knew this was going to be her life. Troy was the only man she would ever love.

He was her other half.

She was both excited and terrified. It would take a while to get her catering business off the ground, but Troy had already found her a few leads at the base.

He was always thinking of her, and that wasn't something she was used to from a boyfriend, but it *was* something she enjoyed.

A lot.

"I never thought I'd see my little girl fall so hard and fast. And for a flyboy," her dad said. "But if I had to handpick a man, he'd be the one."

"I agree," her mother said. "So, we thank you for helping them see they are a match made in heaven."

"They both fought it," Henrietta said.

"You two did come on a little strong," she said with a laugh.

"We had to. We know our son." Henrietta raised her glass. "And after getting to know you, well, we were right."

"Have you told her?" Harold asked.

"Told me what?" It meant the world to her that both sets of parents had become friends. She loved how close Troy's family was and since she lost her brother, her parents had been a little lost. The Bowies had been so welcoming and loving. It warmed her heart.

"We have considered moving up here to Seattle," her father said.

"Really?" Priela blinked. "I wouldn't be opposed to that."

"Good, because we already mentioned it to Troy," her mother interjected.

"We suggested a real estate agent and even suggested some neighborhoods," Harold said. "Family is important and we consider all of you to be ours now."

"Wow. This is unexpected and Troy didn't mention anything to me."

"We wanted to talk with you first," her mother

said. "We don't want to force ourselves on you, especially since it will be three years before you move back, but we want to be near you."

"I want that too," she said.

Troy returned. "Can I get anyone some coffee or tea? Or more wine?"

"I think we're good." Her father had a grin on his face that reminded Priela of the day she'd graduated from the naval academy. It was a prideful look, and whenever he got it, his eyes got shimmery.

"Alrighty then." Troy stuffed one hand into his right pocket and scratched the back of his neck with the other.

Her mother leaned over and snagged a tissue from the box on the table by the sofa and dabbed at the corners of her eyes. She handed the box to Henrietta, who did the same.

"Why do I feel like everyone in this room knows something that I don't?" She glanced from her parents, to Troy's, and then to her boyfriend, who paced nervously in front of the fireplace. Troy rarely got flustered, except for when he had something he wanted to say or ask and he wasn't sure how she'd respond. "Someone better start talking."

Troy took her by the hand and helped her to her feet. "You know I love you."

"Now you're scaring me."

"I'm frightening myself," he mumbled, pulling something out of his pocket. "I know this is crazy and fast, but we're not a conventional couple."

"No, we're not." She blinked, staring at the familiar shiny ring between Troy's thumb and forefinger. "Is that my grandmother's engagement ring?"

"It is," Troy said as he dropped to one knee. "I love you, Priela, and I don't want to just live with you. I want us to be a partnership in every sense of the word." He paused and took in a deep breath.

While she held hers, trying to find the courage to find her voice.

"Will you marry me?" He pressed the ring onto her shaky finger.

She glanced over her shoulder. "Did all of you know about this?"

Henrietta and Harold nodded.

"How do you think he got your grandmother's ring?" Her father waved his hand. "But seriously. Don't leave the man hanging. Give him an answer."

"This certainly isn't how I thought tonight would go." She swiped at the tears burning a hot streak down her cheeks.

"What did you expect?" Troy held her hand

and stared.

"I was prepared for a lot of teasing from our parents, but never in a million years did I think you'd propose marriage in front of them."

"You're killing me here," he whispered. "Do I have to beg?"

"As much fun as that would be, I wouldn't dare make you grovel in front of your dad. He'd never let you live it down." She smiled. "Yes. A thousand times, yes."

Troy stood, wrapping his arms around her and twirling her around.

In Troy's arms, she'd found a home.

Thank you so much for reading FLY AWAY. Next up in the series is FLIRT AWAY, Zane's Story! Please feel free to leave an honest review. I love to hear from readers!

Sign up for my [Newsletter](https://dl.bookfunnel.com/82gm8b9k4y) where I often give away free books before publication.

Join my private [Facebook group](https://www.facebook.com/groups/191706547909047/) where I post exclusive excerpts and discuss all things murder and love!

ABOUT THE AUTHOR

Jen Talty is the *USA Today* Bestselling Author of Contemporary Romance, Romantic Suspense, and Paranormal Romance. In the fall of 2020, her short story was selected and featured in a 1001 Dark Nights Anthology.

Regardless of the genre, her goal is to take you on a ride that will leave you floating under the sun with warmth in your heart. She writes stories about broken heroes and heroines who aren't necessarily looking for romance, but in the end, they find the kind of love books are written about :).

She first started writing while carting her kids to one hockey rink after the other, averaging 170 games per year between 3 kids in 2 countries and 5 states. Her first book, IN TWO WEEKS was originally published in 2007. In 2010 she helped form a publishing company (Cool Gus Publishing) with *NY*

Times Bestselling Author Bob Mayer where she ran the technical side of the business through 2016.

Jen is currently enjoying the next phase of her life…the empty nester! She and her husband reside in Jupiter, Florida.

Grab a glass of vino, kick back, relax, and let the romance roll in…

Sign up for my Newsletter (https://dl.bookfunnel.com/82gm8b9k4y) where I often give away free books before publication.

Join my private Facebook group (https://www.facebook.com/groups/191706547909047/) where I post exclusive excerpts and discuss all things murder and love!

Never miss a new release. Follow me on Amazon:amazon.com/author/jentalty

And on Bookbub: bookbub.com/authors/jentalty

When A Stranger Calls

His Deadly Past

The Corkscrew Killer

Brand New Novella for the First Responders series

A spin-off from the NY State Troopers series

PLAYING WITH FIRE

PRIVATE CONVERSATION

THE RIGHT GROOM

AFTER THE FIRE

CAUGHT IN THE FLAMES

CHASING THE FIRE

Legacy Series

Dark Legacy

Legacy of Lies

Secret Legacy

Emerald City

INVESTIGATE AWAY

SAIL AWAY

Colorado Brotherhood Protectors

The Monroes

COLOR ME YOURS

COLOR ME SMART

COLOR ME FREE

COLOR ME LUCKY

COLOR ME ICE

COLOR ME HOME

Search and Rescue

PROTECTING AINSLEY

PROTECTING CLOVER

PROTECTING OLYMPIA

PROTECTING FREEDOM

PROTECTING PRINCESS

PROTECTING MARLOWE

DELTA FORCE-NEXT GENERATION

SHIELDING JOLENE

SHIELDING AALYIAH

SHIELDING LAINE

SHIELDING TALULLAH

SHIELDING MARIBEL

BURNING KISS

BURNING SKIES

BURNING LIES

BURNING HEART

BURNING BED

REMEMBER ME ALWAYS

The Brotherhood Protectors

Out of the Wild

ROUGH JUSTICE

ROUGH AROUND THE EDGES

ROUGH RIDE

ROUGH EDGE

ROUGH BEAUTY

The Brotherhood Protectors

The Saving Series

SAVING LOVE

SAVING MAGNOLIA

SAVING LEATHER

Hot Hunks

Cove's Blind Date Blows Up

My Everyday Hero – Ledger

Tempting Tavor

Malachi's Mystic Assignment

Needing Neor

Holiday Romances

A CHRISTMAS GETAWAY

ALASKAN CHRISTMAS

WHISPERS

CHRISTMAS IN THE SAND

Heroes & Heroines on the Field

TAKING A RISK

TEE TIME

A New Dawn

THE BLIND DATE

SPRING FLING

SUMMERS GONE

WINTER WEDDING

THE AWAKENING

The Collective Order

THE LOST SISTER

THE LOST SOLDIER

THE LOST SOUL

THE LOST CONNECTION

THE NEW ORDER

www.ingramcontent.com/pod-product-compliance
Lightning Source LLC
Chambersburg PA
CBHW070627100726
47907CB00007B/1893